The Cryptographer's Ink

& Other Stories

Macgregor Douglas

For the 'dented tin.'

CONTENTS

Title Page	1
Copyright	2
Dedication	3
Introduction	7
Laika	13
Chapter 1	14
Chapter 2	16
Chapter 3	19
Chapter 4	23
Chapter 5	26
Monsters	31
Chapter 1	32
Chapter 2	35
Chapter 3	39
Chapter 4	44
Chapter 5	48
The Country Jaunt	55
1	56
2	61
The Cryptographer's Ink	67

Chapter One — 2019   68

Chapter Two — 2006   72

Chapter Three — 2019   77

Chapter Four — 1943   81

Chapter Five — 2019   87

Chapter Six — 1943   93

Chapter Seven — 2019   99

Chapter Eight — 2006   104

Chapter Nine — 2019   109

Chapter Ten — 2019   115

Sìol cluaran   121

1   122

2   124

3   127

4   130

Fear   133

Unholy Chapel   139

Chapter 1   140

Chapter 2   144

Chapter 3   147

Chapter 4   152

Chapter 5   154

Chapter 6   159

Chapter 7   164

Chapter 8   168

Epilogue   173

INTRODUCTION

I was always fascinated, even as a child, at the skill required to create 'short shorts.' I don't mean the kind you might wear at the pool, but the science fiction kind that sometimes lasted only a couple of paragraphs — sometimes less. A story like that has no fat to trim, no unnecessary fluff or filler, just the facts. As a pre-teen with a super short attention span, I found these pieces of writing ideal entertainment. It wasn't until later that I began to appreciate character development and what has become popular in the entertainment industry — the 'slow burn.'

The contents of this book are cobbled together from the same dregs that every 'never-was' writer has hidden away. School exercise books, floppy disks, USB sticks, and abandoned hard-drives that have to be plugged into mains power and sound like vacuum cleaners — our footprints are all over them.

At the risk of sounding like an undeserved and premature Oscar speech, I do want to offer sincere thanks to everyone who generously tolerated my requests to proofread and appraise my numerous drafts of the entries in this volume.

For those ready to just get reading, feel free to skip the next section, it gives a small explanation of the history and birth of each story contained herein.

One powerhouse in the creation, shaping, and completion of much of this content is my wife, Cristina.

Often we'd be discussing the news of the day, a movie, a social media story, etc. and between us, a brainstorm would start for a story idea. Many were basic 'what if' scenarios that went on to play out in either sublime or ridiculous ways. Similar to an excellent song-writing partnership, we'd knock heads and disagree, but this tended to be necessary to hone stories that meandered and pull them back into line.

LAIKA
I wondered what it might be like for the first alien/astronaut contact not to be with a human. Laika, the Soviet dog who, through no fault of her own, was sent into space aboard Sputnik 2, would have communicated exactly as dogs do. As far as we were told, she probably didn't last long outside the atmosphere, terrified and alone. Her oxygen supply was fairly limited and it is thought that she most likely suffocated before burning up during reentry.

So why not give her a more noble death...

MONSTERS
Each generation looks at the fashion and cosmetic choices of those before and those ahead and shakes its head in disbelief. Another late-night spousal discussion turned to possible developments in the search for immortal beauty or the quest for it. Immortality, through cosmetic intervention and even extremes like cryonics, were the subject of Cristina's first doctorate. Anyway, it didn't take long for the story of a dark and frightening future to take form...

THE COUNTRY JAUNT
For all of its imagery of pristine paradisaic environment and friendly peace-loving citizenry, New Zealand still struggles, like many countries, with a secret shame. Domestic violence is rife among certain pockets of the community, and worse, violence toward children. What's even worse still, is that convictions and

sentences handed down for these atrocities are weak, insubstantial, and devalue those young victims' deaths as being of no consequence. Many of the extended family and friends I encountered during my 20s and 30s living in Aotearoa, had been affected directly and indirectly by this.

The story itself is fictional, based on certain people I knew, and of the several victims in this story, most have a satisfactory resolution, one does not.

THE CRYPTOGRAPHER'S INK
There's intrigue, mystery, and triumph over adversity. There's also human ingenuity, empathy, and sacrifice.

One key motivating factor in this story is that I despise war — think M*A*S*H times infinity. The most difficult task was the writing of the war scenes. At one point I even approached a fellow author to ask if he'd write them for me if I gave him an outline. In the end, I figured that I couldn't really get into the headspace of my protagonist if I didn't live the war with him, so I did.

Dementia features in the body of this story as it zips back-and-forth through time. I've used a little license in some of the stereotypes about the disease, but for the most part, have tried to remain true to the characters and their associated behaviours.

SÌOL CLUARAN
There are three radically different drafts of this story, and I am sure Cristina would be happy to point out that she steered me away from disaster with the first two. They read more like a high school science history essay.

In the end, I came around and started basically from scratch with the character-driven story of a botanist and an orphan boy who may have survived the cataclysm, only to suffer a similar fate.

FEAR
This is probably my shortest ever story, but I wanted to include it as it raises some very worrying questions about medical ethics as we look to the future.

UNHOLY CHAPEL
I have had this sitting as a finished graphic novel (without graphics) for over a decade. I wrote it out in long-form and then my wife got her hands on it and told me all the things that were missing. OK, it was only a couple of things - but she was right, as usual.

I have had to force myself not to become too enamoured with stories of vigilantism, as it is a concept I find hard not to be drawn to. I've written a couple of different stories with this bent, so from that group, this is the one I have chosen to include.

Macgregor Douglas - June 2020

LAIKA

CHAPTER 1

The Laern spacecraft moved silently in the dark places.

They had long since learned from millennia of failed missions at the hands of hostile 'civilizations' to stay hidden and to assess a people carefully, before initiating contact. Thus, a method had been perfected in which the ship's computers kept them invisible, hovering in the blackness between stars when viewed from the planet's surface.

Aboard, were mostly cross-skilled professionals, pilots, navigators, engineers, botanists, medical personnel, geneticists, mathematicians and statisticians, chemists, and theoretical physicists — cosmologists all. Gone were the scorned days of *rank*, a concept which to most brought a scornful humourless chuckle, as if pitying the societal immaturity of generations past.

From this number, two were at the scanning console, conducting a 27º forward sweep as they drifted toward the attractive solar system dead ahead.

Technology had become almost organic in the hundred years leading up to their current mission. They performed the most complex functions of the powerful sensor array with precise gestures of their reedlike, graceful limbs, interpreted by light-sensitive electronic 'eyes' and converted in a flash to mechanical actions.

Vertus, slightly taller than his colleague, Loquin, made an inquisitive grunt to catch the other's attention and spread the digits of his left 'hand' slowly — a gesture which expanded the view on-screen and brought into focus what appeared to be a tiny, irregular metal object.

"Technology?" Loquin inquired, tilting his head to regard Vertus. Although devoid of any feature beyond his own unique and identifiable tinge, Vertus was quickly able to interpret Loquin's emotion by the pattern of ripples that radiated from the centre of his face. At this time, the glassy pool showed a gentle undulating of youthful curiosity, with a respectful hint of humility that went with addressing an elder Laern.

Vertus replied matter-of-factly: "Probably just a metal-rich asteroid that's gone renegade from that belt between the fifth and sixth orbits, I shouldn't wonder. But we'll need to mark it for closer examination in case it needs to be cleared from our path."

He had barely finished speaking when text started to appear in the top right-hand corner of the screen. The flowing ellipsoidal characters of their written language joined into each other with wisps, reminiscent both of the outer arms of spiral galaxies and the Laerns' anatomical extremities. This similarity was by no means accidental.

"Vertus!" Loquin cried, "this is no rock — we've detected life! The signal indicates that the life-form is experiencing significant distress. Perhaps we can reach it in time to render aid?"

Ignoring his young companion's elevated level of excitement, Vertus was already putting a call through to the main flight deck, requesting a minor course change to intercept the small vehicle.

CHAPTER 2

"This is Pitri, reporting from the interior of the alien satellite. We found the traveller weak, unconscious and in a state of severe depletion of its primary mainstays — oxygen for respiration, and a liquid compound of hydrogen/oxygen to nourish its body at a cellular level. We have provided temporary relief until we can establish contact and determine how she, a female by our anatomical reckoning, came to be in this predicament. They are a carbon-based species, like us and quadrupedal. They suckle their young, and like many of the peoples we have encountered in this region of space, they have all of their sensory organs — olfactory, visual, auditory, and speech — located in their heads. There is no evidence of organs that allow conscious body temperature regulation, although they seem only slightly warmer than our norm. This is partly down to a pelt of naturally grown keratin, which traps the body heat and reflects a lot of it inward to maintain warmth. The patient is stirring, I will report shortly with more information..."

"... This is Hoizl. While Pitri tends to the alien, I am examining the vessel's technology. Basic, yes — childishly so — yet I think it belies a civilization in its infancy that is experiencing a technological growth spurt. I imagine less than a century of planetary revolutions around this star, and they'll be heading outward in faster-than-light colony ships. There seems a distinct lack of readout or written material on board, although the external shell bears pageantry and markings that look like lingual representation. I am transmitting visuals as you can see."

Простейший Спутник 2.

"Also, the alien herself has a lingual representation in the same style attached to her neck."

Лайка.

"I have discovered a receptacle that dispenses food. Each time the button is depressed to activate it, there is an accompanying audio message — I have forwarded this also for you to hear how it sounds phonetically: *Khoroshaya Devochka, Laika.* Pitri surmises that 'Laika' may be the personal name of the cosmonaut as she has responded immediately to it with alertness since awakening…"

"… Pitri again; Laika has revived and seems hugely grateful and elated to have been rescued. She has a delightful method of greeting — gently caressing with an appendage that emerges from her organ of speech — and it seems to match exactly with pleasure centres of her central nervous system and endocrine release mechanisms. Both Hoizl and myself agree on experiencing a 'healthy euphoria' that results from her company. She seems well aware of the main panel in front of her and shows immense curiosity at the surrounding space insofar as can be seen directly through the viewing plate. It is a mystery as to why, despite having muscular limbs suitable for ambulation, she has been secured in place in a manner that she is unable to free herself, although the volume of the cabin prevents wider movement anyway. As yet, we have failed to establish commonalities of even the most basic communication. This is frustrating, as it is obvious she wants to open dialogue…"

"… This is Hoizl again; as you have heard from Pitri, the task of learning Laika's languages is one that will require more than guessing games and drawing numbers and shapes in the air. Hence, assuming your unanimous accord, we have a suggestion: her vessel won't survive another day, by their planet's standard, and there's no way to patch it up enough for it to survive the reentry trip and land safely. We propose transporting her via stealth-shuttle to her point of origin upon the largest landmass of the fourth planet and to monitor her reception via a microscopic video transmitter we can painlessly attach adjacent to her ocular organs. In this way, we can see Laika's interactions with fellows of her own kind and plan our first official visit more appropriately, especially as she will have already explained to them about how she was rescued and about our diplomacy…"

CHAPTER 3

Vertus, Loquin, and every nonessential crew-member aboard watched with barely contained anticipation as the first visuals started coming through to the giant screen in their spacecraft's capacious viewing hall.

They'd waited and watched as the intrepid traveller was fitted obediently with a video transmitter, sedated, and moved to the streamlined bubble of a stealth shuttle. The ill-fated alien satellite had disintegrated close to the atmosphere of its home planet shortly afterwards. It was during this intra-atmospheric spectacle that the shuttle had slid through undetected and made its way to the surface. It arrived within a short distance of the very spot from which Laika had lifted off only days before. Designed to quickly dissolve and disperse in the atmosphere, no trace of the stealth-shuttle would be found by the inhabitants of the planet when they eventually discovered the lone female cosmonaut.

With Laika's returning consciousness came the first images.

Initially, the focus was poor, reflective of the gradual awakening process and they could only make out blurred shapes circling her, occasionally pausing to come closer and then returning to the vigil. As the scene came into sharper contrast, they could see that two other aliens were excitedly interacting with Laika using the same caressing greeting that Pitri and Hoizl had experienced during their first contact. The variations in their appearance were evident, the keratin layer of one had a pale, neutral colour all over, and she bore a different symbology at her neck: Албина. The second was similar, but with dark patches surrounding her organs of sight. She moved in an erratic pattern, frequently spinning around and leaping in the air. Still, they managed to catch sight of her designation eventually as she came closer and appeared to be testing Laika's odour with the moist olfactory organ at the foremost extremely of her face: *Мушка*.

After a short time, the trio started to move. All three were now mobile and travelling quickly through vegetation and long grasses punctuated with clumps of frozen gas, which slowly gave way to geometric structures, buildings, and more examples of machinery and technology.

Suddenly, the scene went dark, and they realized that the trio had entered one of the buildings and was now trotting easily along corridors that must be familiar to them. Coming to a final entry point, the two companions sat back on their hind limbs and appeared to be seeking ingress by throwing their heads back and shouting. Presently, the barrier slid aside, and the Laern onlookers were greeted by the sight of an entirely new species. Bipedal and standing fully erect, these unique creatures appeared startled and frightened to see Laika alive and well. This was magnified by the fact that Laika, true to form, seemed ecstatic to see them and danced around them, trying to reach their faces to caress them in greeting.

At first, they stepped back, gesticulating wildly, and then grasped each other's arms and simultaneously covered their organs of speech. After a period of doing this, three of them took up cords of some kind of textile with nooses at one end and quickly passed these over the heads of Laika and her friends. Dragging them harshly further into the complex, the bipeds imprisoned them in barred metal cages. The Laern, having started already to interpret emotions in the shapes of the sight organs of the quadrupeds, stirred uncomfortably as they recognized sudden fright, anxiety, fear, and apprehension.

The silence of the auditorium was split with an exclamation

from the indignant Loquin:

"Can't we help them! They're obviously under attack from these other *monsters* — what are they doing to them?"

Looking around the spacious room, Vertus could see that Loquin had merely echoed the thoughts of everyone present.

From one of the front rows close to the screen, one of the elder crew-members, a venerable historian called Reldus, stood up, bringing a halt to the hubbub that had arisen. All bodies turned in his direction, and he observed a wave of deference sweep through the faces of the crowd, from the outer edges of the group toward him, culminating eventually in a scene that was still and serene as they awaited his wisdom.

"All too easily in the past, we have prejudged a drama upon the tiniest observed sleights, dismissing the players, either to their demise, or choosing it for them, lest they infect other civilized realms."

A low chirp could be heard as many offered a *sotto voce* affirmation of his statement. He went on:

"I am as taken as the rest of you with Laika, her wonderful personality and desire to see her come to no harm. And it is so, too, with her kind, who individually greet her with the same concern and affection; I no more want them to come to harm than I do any of you. But let us observe further before we draw our conclusions. The video transmitter functions well, and I am sure she senses our presence and draws comfort from knowing we are with her, observing everything she experiences. Let us see more — we will adjourn to our various duties and reconvene here when notified of any further relevant activity."

Somewhat calmed by his words, the busy scientists dispersed to their various workstations and laboratories, trying unsuccessfully to relegate the precious Laika to the backs of their minds for a few hours. This was especially difficult for those who were off shift and had to gather in small clusters around recreation pools. They quietly shared recordings of Pitri's first encounter, basking in the shared vibrations that it engendered. This feature of their physiology negated envy or jealousy, as an emotional experience could be shared as easily amongst two or three Laern, as it could a million. The myriad sensations of unclouded joy, friendship, humility, gratitude, and companionship that had passed from Laika to Pitri and Hoizl, now spread and flowed through the ship like plant spores.

Yet they could not help feeling troubled by the disturbing imagery they had all witnessed.

CHAPTER 4

A blinking alarm on each console alerted them that there was a change, and with renewed enthusiasm and resolve the Laern family, for indeed they considered all in their midst to be so, again returned to share the visual drama as it unfolded before them. This time, some of the more practical and logical amongst them tied their computer stations into the video, in case they might capture useful stills for analysis in more detail.

Laika and her fellows had settled somewhat but still sat with the greeting appendages hanging limply from their speech organs and the trunks of their small bodies expanding and contracting with elevated respiration as they observed the comings and goings of the bipeds. The stress levels presently appeared to rise again in the faces of her companions, and they shouted and spun themselves in circles as Laika was removed from her cage and borne to another part of the room toward a high steel table. She was held down and immobilized there by more of the tight cords, then flooded with blinding lights that caused much discomfort as she writhed her head from side to side, struggling to avoid them. Presently one of her captors moved the lights to her abdomen, which had now been draped with sheets manufactured from plant fibres. This individual bore the appearance of a medical technician, judging by the primitive-looking tools it selected from a nearby rack. It was soon joined by three other bipeds of varying body shapes, possibly indicating variations in gender. All had masked their faces with fibrous squares, probably to prevent breathing in unknown toxins or microbes from the hapless patient.

The Laern audience felt paralyzed, new waves of nausea sweeping over them as they saw Laika's body attacked with fine metallic needles pushed under the skin, delivering several different coloured liquids and likewise drawing fluids from her circulatory system. Others used sharp blades to cut away the keratin covering and then cut deeper, taking samples of her flesh away. The vicarious pain responses of the Laern crew-members caused many to cry out, seeing Laika growing weaker as she tried to wriggle free and away from the torturous implements being used upon her.

Eventually, the reprieve came as the bipeds drifted one by one away through other doors, some bearing droplets and splashes of Laika's life liquids upon their garments. The initial technician poured something from a container onto a small piece of the fabric and moved to Laika's head. For a moment, unbelievably, he put his palm out as if making a sign of affection. The pink flesh of her greeting appendage reached toward the hand and stroked it weakly. Then, the moment was over. The fabric was swathed around her olfactory organ and held there despite her pitiful attempt to resist. Gradually, the screen resolved to blank as she fell unconscious.

Unable to withstand the boiling mixture of emotions that assaulted them, some of the audience had left the hall in disgust, and many felt unwell in their cores. Reldus himself was among their number, and another elder Laern stood in his place to announce that they would observe for two more revolutions of the planet and then a definitive course of action would be decided.

For many Laern crew-members, the only solace they could draw upon was to replay the first contact chronicles, yet they found the comforting cold, in light of the atrocities they had seen.

The biologists among them, along with language specialists, ethnologists, and historians, remained alert to every instance of consciousness that Laika experienced. They recorded the environment and any examples of symbols and writing they came across. Others analyzed the crude transmissions from various alien sources at the surface. These seemed dominated by the media of the bipedal species, and it became increasingly apparent that they had oppressed Laika's species and probably suppressed their ability to broadcast between themselves. As yet unable to decode Laika's language, they had no way of telling if they were perhaps visitors from another world who had been ambushed by the bipeds and then subjugated.

CHAPTER 5

Shortly before the end of the second cycle, this small group witnessed the most upsetting events of all and demanded a reconvention of the assembly ahead of the appointed decision deadline. The multitude materialized instantly, and its members took their places without comment. One of the scientists started the playback of what they had themselves already just seen.

As Laika awoke, it became apparent that each of her friends had suffered similarly at the hands of their captors. They each lay wrapped loosely in a single slip of light fabric that was blotched all over with circulatory fluid. Some of the liquid was congealed, yet other wounds dripped and suppurated freely. The captors no longer bothered to separate the quadrupeds into different cages, given their complete lack of mobility. The Laern observed that, even in their wretched state, the three imprisoned creatures made tender efforts to relieve the injuries of each other, gently stroking them with their multi-purpose greeting appendages.

Before long, the companion with the dark facial patterns lapsed into unconsciousness. Despite the attempts of the others to revive her, she did not move again. As the concerned viewers looked on from the spaceship thousands of miles above, her respiration slowed and then stopped altogether.

Unable to escape from the giant view screen, each Laern felt inexorably held in place, aware of an impending end, yet unable to look away.

Laika, sensing that only one friend could now be cared for, wriggled painfully closer, and with an effort lifted her right forward limb, letting it rest across the neck of the other. Even at this great distance, the Laern assembly could sense the shared comfort of the two creatures in the face of such insurmountable conditions.

Time passed, measured only by the transient shadows of ignorant passersby falling over the prone bodies, not once pausing to glance in on them, even for a moment.

Finally, mercifully, the camera swept to the ceiling and became still as Laika's head lolled back and the video signal dimmed with her consciousness. A last electrical static spark fizzed across the screen, and it went blank, letting the silent multitude know that life had been extinguished from her little body.

For a long moment, a tangible pall hung in the air overhead, threatening to suck the breath from every person. Each felt struck by the sudden solitude they felt, despite the proximity of their closest colleagues. Slowly, they once again became aware of the presence of Reldus, who had inconspicuously taken centre stage.

Rather than speak, Reldus motioned toward a female in the small group of scientists who had insisted on sharing the events they had just witnessed. She gestured toward her console, and still-images were displayed on the main screen.

"We don't want to depersonalize this event, but we also need to act quickly and decisively in a short time. Please note: here is a frame showing the biped's written language, as seen on the plant fibre sheets they use to record on. Yes, it is hanging upside down as the female biped holds it in front of the cage, but there is sufficient material for our coding programs to decipher a translation. It reads:

'... *international repercussions of a seemingly supernatural occurrence are untenable, and the evidence must be destroyed immediately following genetic sampling and extensive internal organ biopsy. Total incineration of all participants recommended, irrespect-*

ive of whether they were chosen to participate, or not. We cannot risk leakage of any secret information about Laika, Albina, or Mushka; lest it should draw unwanted American interest and raise frictions we are eager to avoid…'"

A somewhat more rotund scientist on her left, missing a left limb altogether, took over.

"Now look at this second piece of evidence. You will see here a series of media frames, transmitted via low frequencies across this planet. We have compiled images of the treatment of not only quadrupedal species including Laika's; but also thousands of others, many hunted and killed for nothing more than endorphin stimulation activity among the bipeds. This slaughter is not limited to other species either; they also engage in the individual and mass killing of their own."

He made a broad sweep across the entire group with his one functional limb:

"It would seem to us that with such a short time to decide for the preservation of helpless peoples like the huge variety of quadrupeds inhabiting this world in relative harmony, we need to eradicate the biped species without delay."

Reldus continued the momentum of the discussion:

"What of the sacred texts of the bipeds you were endeavouring to decipher?"

"Time hasn't been on our side, and we have only crudely translated the beginning portion. It seems *the bipeds' deity destroyed them* at the infancy of their civilization in favour of preserving the many other species. This is reflected in the sacred or historical writings of dozens of different cultures. Details are indistinct, but unfortunately, it seems that some bipeds survived and again bred to the extent that they became the dominant and most violent, death-dealing people."

To avoid an undue lapse into speculation, Reldus spoke up abruptly: "You know me. I can't abide death in any form, but I also feel that the rule of Protection Of The Innocent And Oppressed, applies here. Long ago, we had only one method of dealing with insidious diseases of our organism, and that was to cut them out. Likewise indeed, when one people became so unhealthy and aberrant in their behaviour toward another, it was, and still is, considered an act of kindness to put them out of their misery and in so doing restore safety and order to the rest."

He paused a moment, then went on:

"Still I say: let any one of those here today who disagrees, speak up without fear of reprisal and we shall pause the decision."

As was customary, each Laern turned to face their fellow on one side, sharing a carefully straight facial ripple that descended from the crown of their head until it disappeared into their chin. Then, turning to the other, they repeated the ritual, remaining in absolute silence. One by one they faced again toward the front, bowing their heads solemnly without a word.

The Laern spacecraft moved silently in the dark places.

MONSTERS

Copyright © May 2018

Inspired from an original concept by Cristina Douglas

CHAPTER 1

A ripple of excitement spread through the gathered crowd who remained almost entirely silent despite having no such constraint laid upon them. Squeezed shoulder to shoulder into the cramped viewing lounge, with the tallest at the back and some kneeling in the front row, they jostled one another with hands smothering the explosion of suppressed giggles. Eyes flashed and bulged in anticipation of the voyeuristic titillations to come.

Their faces glowed with the bright reflection of the scene from the room below them. It was a relatively luxurious hotel room, expensively appointed with thick draperies and natural wood paneling that complemented the richly upholstered furniture. The carpet was soft and pale, with occasional textured rugs sprawled before them, uninterrupted, save for the monarch sized bed centered in the feature wall.

The feature wall was oriented to the left of the onlookers, and they were able to observe the lone occupant full-length, from her head on the pillow right down to her feet. Still sleeping and facing away from their position, she gave away hints of life only in the gentle rise and fall of a milky white shoulder and the arm that held the satin cover around her. Her shape, too, was a pleasing one, enhanced in the eyes of the viewers by the bubbling wines in their veins and by the proximity of other young bodies in the tight space. Many hands seemed to have inadvertently fallen to adjacent thighs, arms or waists and remained there, unchallenged — heightening the thrill of the moment.

A whispered voice that they recognized instantly as that of their host galvanized them to rapt attention.

"I'm going to try and wake her, but I'll be gentle."

Allowed now to hear an audio feed from the room, a more intense hush came over them as they collectively held their breath. They became aware of the morning song of birds, gradually increasing in volume and fading to a dull diegetic background.

The woman stirred. She stretched slowly and gracefully. The underside of one foot peeked from under the sheet. She had an abundance of thick, gorgeous hair that lay clinging to the satin bedclothes as if charged with static electricity. It undulated back and forth with the movement of her body like soft seaweed in the tide's clutches. This only served to send fresh chills into the extremities of the secret audience.

A number of them gasped with carnal delight as she suddenly rolled toward them onto her back, casting the top sheet to her waist and letting her hand rest on her exposed belly. Her hair still wholly obscured her face and neck, but only partially covered her ample breasts. Not surprisingly, this made the tension even more excruciating for the party-goers.

A hoarse whisper came from one of the male members of the group.

"Zoom in! Come on, zoom!"

The host reached to his control pad and made a swirling gesture over the zoom icon. The recumbent woman's body eased closer to fill the window until only the upper body from head to knees could be seen. The image was so clear that the tiny goosebumps on her skin, and even the hairs that made them, was easily discerned.

Without warning, she sat up quickly, with one fluid motion. She tossed her head, flinging the hair out of her face and turned to look directly at the large Ashley Shaw print on the ceiling diagonally opposite, unaware of its transparency from the soundproofed chamber beyond.

And just as well. The panicked shrieks and sudden clamoring to get as far from the window as possible was almost deafening in the small room. Arms flailed. One collision after another occurred as the none-too-sober rabble ran half-euphoric, half-terrified into the much larger dining hall where they had previously spent most of the evening.

Once there, they fell against one other in uncontrolled gales of laughter, trying desperately to regain their breath after the sudden shock and subsequent adrenaline rush. Driven by the ultra-sensuality of the experience, many fell to indiscriminate fondling and passionate making out.

As the atmosphere calmed and everyone finally stood regarding each other across the room with flushed, rosy expressions and tousled hair and clothes, the preposterously wealthy host finally spoke up.

"Make sure that when you invite your unsuspecting friends next month, you say absolutely *nothing* about what they're going to see, OK. I'm sure it was worth waiting for without the spoiler — agreed?"

The hot-blooded young men and women looked around the room at each other, smiling and nodding conspiratorially.

It had been worth every penny.

It had been worth the wait.

CHAPTER 2

"Mom, it just didn't work that way anymore, the way it used to. I kept getting passed up because I'd missed the boat."

Courtney Pippin brushed her jet-black fringe from her eyes and took a slow drag from a half-smoked cigarette in the same hand. The other held a smartphone, the screen semi-lit with her mother's avatar. Her forearm rested comfortably on a small al fresco restaurant table.

It was a quiet afternoon, the sun was low in the sky, creating broad streaks of blood-orange and vermillion through the sparse clouds and a cool breeze rustled the leaves of the Hollywood Boulevard palm trees.

Her mother's voice droned from the Bluetooth earpiece offering platitudes that were genuine, yet all too familiar from her limited arsenal of emotional support. The older woman had understood little of the vagaries of the celebrity milieu — opting instead, as so many parents did, to believe that their son or daughter was just as deserving to be famous as the next person. Of course, she'd had good reason to feel this way back in the day in Courtney's case.

Courtney Pippin had been a star, gracing the living rooms of more than half the world in her heyday and making the not-always-effortless transition smoothly into blockbuster film acting. Even though a lot of her fortune had gone into the sponsorship of several charitable foundations of which she was patron and spokeswoman, she still found herself yearning for the camera's attention.

What she hadn't bargained on was *Gniega* — the miracle drug.

In the early 20s, the Biotech Centre for Enhanced Mortality, a British conglomerate of top researchers in the field of rejuvenation and longevity, chanced upon some revolutionary footage of stem cell interaction with living tissues that had been damaged by Hutchinson-Gilford syndrome and Werner syndrome. A combination of particular electrical conditions in conjunction with a primordial amniotic-type catalyst had yielded incredible results. The damaged dermal structure had been utterly restored and continued to hold in what was considered to be the most stable state of youthful elasticity possible for human adult skin.

With lightning speed, the discovery was synthesized into a serum that could be mixed into water and taken orally, yielding astonishing results in as little as two months. Thus, *Gniega* was born.

As yet, out of astronomical cost only affordable to the super-wealthy, the new drug had taken the celebrity universe by storm, with unexpected and distressing results. No one could have suspected that the side-effects would manifest with such irony, with such a cruel and painful twist of fate.

A fate that had almost befallen Courtney and had affected many, many of her peers.

At the height of her young career, Courtney Pippin was arguably one of the top ten most beautiful women in Western media. She had an ideal model's build, smooth, unblemished complexion with sharp cheekbones, classically striking contrast of very dark hair with porcelain features and a mischievously upturned slash of a mouth that people, old or young, male or female found themselves drawn to. She could be cute, innocent, smart, and sultry at the same time in a way that never came across as cheap or offensive. Audiences adored her, and there was no shortage of eager industry sycophants waiting to join the ride.

But underneath the confident facade lay the same insecurities and pressures of vanity that had plagued women and men of fame for centuries. Courtney fell prey to the shallow musings of media critics and glamour 'experts' who demanded constant perfection from all celebrities.

It started with small procedures — a collagen injection here, a brow-lift there, electrolysis, and regular peels. As time went on and the relentless focus remained unabated, Courtney succumbed to more invasive interventions. Her teeth became almost painfully white and so straight that they looked *too* perfect. Her usually delicate slight frame was suddenly burdened with a pair of augmented breasts that altered her entire posture and way of walking and gesturing. Simultaneously, the accompanying wardrobe adjustments went from tastefully sexy sweaters and tops to suddenly garish outfits with plunging frontages that seemed tailored only to expose the new structures into a tightly bulging cleavage that left nothing to the imagination.

As the months rolled on, she started to suffer both physical and emotional problems, from developing back pain to despondency and depression. Unable to stop the perpetual motion of her plastic surgery addiction, she had various reshaping procedures on her nose, eyes, and chin. And on the recommendation of fellow cast members, she had botox injections to try and mitigate lines and wrinkles around her upper lip. This resulted in the lamentable situation that so many had discovered — the ability to take flawless publicity shots for magazine covers, but the total inability to show any facial expression with that part of the mouth. In onscreen conversations, her upper lip started to look like a piece of dead cardboard, unmoving and definitely. not. natural.

Ever gracious, Courtney had turned her experience into an opportunity to speak out for younger generations of actors and actresses, encouraging them to embrace their flaws and to grow with dignity, avoiding the ravages of cosmetic intervention. And when *Gniega* came along — it seemed that her pleas were to be heeded. As a demonstration of solidarity, Courtney had herself made a stand against using the new anti-aging miracle.

Three things happened.

The new blood started taking *Gniega* and continued to look fantastic.

The much older generation of acting royalty, who had elected to remain as nature intended and grow old, started taking *Gniega* and astoundingly began to look decades younger. They even found themselves once again in demand professionally.

And... the generation of artificial beauty — Courtney's generation — started taking *Gniega*.

CHAPTER 3

The creeps on the corner of West 143rd Street and Hamilton Place made it impossible for Heidi to take the easy route to work.

Even with her baggy sweats and generous hood, she couldn't chance a confrontation that might expose her and risk severe ridicule, a beating, or some worse form of abuse. The horror stories were rampant through the motley crew of colleagues she spent her nights with. One guy had been hung up over an NBC billboard — upside down so that passersby could stop and see his face clearly. When his friends finally found him and cut him down, they found he'd had a chisel inserted into the vertebra between his shoulder blades and had been dead for hours. Members of both sexes had been raped and left for dead at different times, and both local police and federal authorities seemed inclined to avoid more than cursory investigations.

A widespread attitude had settled upon the masses, accompanied by a closed-minded apathy toward her kind: they did it to themselves and, therefore, shouldn't feel shocked when it happened to them. Heidi shivered as this ever-familiar train of thought entered her mind once again. It was just like the pervading attitude during the decades either side of the turn of the millennium that posited: *any young woman being harassed or even molested by an attacker, was 'asking for it' if she wore provocative clothing and makeup*. As well-intentioned as this advice might have seemed coming from a concerned parent or community spokesperson, the epithet still gave unwarranted license to muggers and rapists, by removing some of the blame from them for their actions and placing it upon the victims.

Heidi mused grimly over how that pseudo-wisdom had mutated over the years. She didn't crave pity or charity for her condition. Like most others of her tribe, she'd accepted that no one could have predicted the tragic results of *Gniega* upon the flesh of humans. Humans that had faces made, effectively, out of their own scar tissue.

As alarm bells had started ringing and plastic surgery telephone exchanges and complaints inboxes had started choking up with angered messages, the world had begun to get the first glimpses of a horror fit for a Stephen King novel. The first few newscasts were just of celebrities running awkwardly from buildings to waiting vehicles, their heads covered with coats or thick scarves, and dozens of security men warding off the ravenous paparazzi. But, inevitably, images had started popping up in media new feeds of the true extent of vanity calling in her debts. Unprepared for the global phenomena of panic and fear, the celebrity media as an industry had virtually crumbled overnight, and a restructured version had not emerged for almost 18 months after the advent of what came to be known as the outbreak of 'The Full Dorian Gray Effect.'

A prominent member of the Biotech Center for Enhanced Mortality, Dr. Robert Andrews, posted a viral video of why *The Effect* had come about. He showed a flat piece of latex rubber of the type used to make party balloons, on which he had drawn a familiar 'have a nice day' smiley face. He mimicked the natural aging process of skin by gently bunching the balloon material to imitate wrinkles — especially around the eyes and upper lips. Next, he emulated cosmetic surgery, by gently swabbing a mild plasticizer into the areas most affected by the wrinkles, until the rubber relaxed again into the flat of the table. This seemed to restore the smiley its former glory until Dr. Andrews asked his assistant to take hold of the opposite side of the rubber sheet from himself and stretch it out between them with a hand at each corner. This, he advised, was *Gniega* as it evenly restored *all* skin of the face to its usual elasticity.

The effect had been both comical and hideous in an all-too-recognizable way. The smiley face was no longer in perfect proportion, with the spots where the chemical 'surgery' had been applied, now creating solid anchor points that twisted deep creases between them as the rubber around them pulled taut, forging bizarre, unnatural angles.

Thus had been the fate of thousands of cosmetically altered faces. With the neutral impartiality of its simple enzyme structure, *Gniega* tore at the scarred eyes, noses, lips, and chins of famous icons everywhere. Some split and left even more deep scars — others merely created garish caricatures of life: some clownish, some monstrous, others demonic.

Leaving the backstreets to cross the last few blocks to the Museum, Heidi quickened her pace and slipped unnoticed down the side alley to the rear staff-only entrance. Safely inside, she stowed her duffle bag in her locker and began changing into her costume. Several others were also in various stages of coming off their shifts or preparing to start work. Her friend Gloria approached and used the low bench in front of the lockers to buckle up a silvery platform-soled shoe. It matched the very artificial skin-tight bodysuit she was wearing, accessorized with a feathery wrap around her neck.

She said, without interrupting her routine: "I hear Mick almost didn't make it home last night, Babe; he tripped in a drain and twisted his ankle. He was lucky his building-Super saw him from the car on his way home and rescued him. He said a bunch of punks had kicked him in the ribs and then ran off to get reinforcements and a camera. *Animals!*"

Gloria spat the last word but failed to hide the moistness of her eyes as she turned away to find a lipstick from the miscellaneous collection the museum left out on a table for them each week. Mentally steeling herself to the task, Heidi brushed ineffectually at the creases in her outfit and then followed Gloria and twelve others through to an anteroom, beyond which lay a large exhibition room. It was swathed in darkness except for several gaudy spotlights that weakly illuminated security-glass display cabinets, placed at intervals around the walls. Splitting up, the individual members of the troupe each followed a narrow corridor to a booth and stepped out from behind a black curtain. Each enclosure contained a waist-height bar stool, upon which its occupant took his or her place to spend the next few hours sitting, unmoving, as the world ogled.

Heidi tried to find a headspace that took her far away from the reality of the human zoo she worked in, but she found herself thinking of Mick's experiences from the night before. Reports like this came in with more frequency every month, keeping the troupe on edge. It caused each to question why the hell they agreed to demean themselves with this crazy type of 'performance art for the perverted,' which in recent years had come to be accepted by the mainstream as an unsavory yet tolerable form of exploitation. She realized that, besides these *Freak-fests*, there were very few jobs that Dorian Effect victims could get.

In such a short time, they'd become social outcasts and objects of curiosity and ridicule — brought on mainly by the high-minded posturing of a select group of celebrities who'd made life a thousand times worse for their fellows. These still believed in their invincibility and superiority over a public that they considered to worship them as it always had. The unfortunate souls had incurred the vehement anger and aggression of the broader population with utterly no shred of mercy. And instead of spearheading the elevated moral exposure of bigotry, the media had jumped *en masse* onto the blame-wagon. Reports about the virtually overnight polar shift from adoration to the abomination of celebrities asserted that if they had displayed even the tiniest bit of modesty and decorum, then the course of history could likely have been very different.

Without the slightest warning, Heidi felt the wind knocked out of her as a powerful arm went across her chest, and a hand came around the other side of her head, totally covering her nose and mouth. She was dragged noiselessly off the stool and behind the curtain, feeling the air rush past as she was carried swiftly back down the corridor. As she squirmed to glance at her surroundings, a small, vile-smelling sack was pulled over her head, and she felt the sharp sting of a syringe under her left ear. She blacked out, barely aware of her heels being hooked off her feet as she was pulled through the side-door of a waiting van.

The van gunned its engines and sped away into the New York night, leaving in its wake only a cloud of exhaust, the fetid tang of burnt tire-rubber, and an abandoned pair of ladies' patent leather high-heeled shoes sitting in the gutter.

CHAPTER 4

Ancient timbers splintered under the intense pressure of two heavyset bodies shouldering their way through the wide entrance doors. Dust from the cracked wooden door panels swirled haphazardly in the vast hallway, picked out in moonbeams that cascaded from several oculi set at intervals in the high ceiling as the two detectives stepped into the mansion with weapons drawn.

With tacit agreement to move further into the building, the older of the pair holstered his gun and twisted his police flashlight until it shone forth a tight, narrow beam. Without looking directly at the other man, he said: "Vince; I'm getting the feeling you know exactly what we're looking for in this dump. How about you let your partner in on the deal?"

Vincent Cox kept his vintage 9 millimeter Beretta moving in a slow sweep ahead of himself as he began to move toward the far end of the entrance hall where flights of stairs curved upwards to the left and right and a further set flowed down in the center to lower levels.

"Remember that byline I showed you last month about the 50th anniversary of the last Dorian dying, George?"

"Yeah... vaguely — those poor bastards had a pretty shit time of it if I remember my history."

"Well, what if I said I don't think they're all *gone* in the strictest sense?"

George Van Helden stopped his progress toward the stairs and shone the light in his friend's face, dazzling him momentarily. Vincent, without saying more, punctuated his question only with a raising of his eyebrows. He resumed his walk to the head of the descending staircase and gestured: "Down here."

As he cast the flashlight back and forth into the mansion's depths, George pondered the nuances of his partner's question. After all, *Gniega* might make everyone look pretty much in the prime of their adult lives, but it sure as hell didn't make them live any longer.

The shameful historical period that had come to be known as the Dorian 'debacle' had gone down in the books alongside the various racial and religious genocides of the nineteenth and twentieth centuries and the horrendous immigration pogroms of post-Trump America. As each generation merged from one to the next, they claimed to have ushered in a new era of human enlightenment, with the evils of the past serving only as a way to shed contrast upon the moral superiority of the present.

They found a wagon wheel configuration of five corridors at the foot of the stairs leading diagonally away from them like spokes. Vincent lifted his nose slightly and then asked:

"What do you smell, George?"

"Well, my nose isn't that great. Incense... maybe?"

"Could be, but if I were a betting man, I'd say it's a mix of stale colognes and perfumes, like you get after a party, you know — mixed with body odor and food."

"Is that significant?" George quizzed him.

Vincent echoed his earlier sentiment: "Could be."

Methodically, they tried each door along the first passageway, as it seemed to be the direction from which the residual smells were strongest. Most were simple, unremarkable bed chambers, with ensuite bathrooms. Close to the end, however, they found a reinforced metal door with no apparent lock or handle of any kind.

"My guess is it's an elevator," said George. "I've seen this kind of thing before, hold on."

Handing the flashlight to Vincent, he took a Swiss army knife from his coat pocket and opened the primary blade. Tapping the wall next to the metal door until he located the hollowest part, he jabbed the sharp implement into it and had soon cut a ragged opening. Vincent shone the bright light into the little space and smiled in muted admiration at a rainbow of coiled wires that terminated at an electrical circuit board. In a flash, George had switched the blade for scissors and stripped three of them, first tying a green wire to a brown one and vice versa and then, leaning backward as if expecting sparks, cutting a black and white striped filament. They were rewarded with a dull, mechanical crunch, which emanated somewhere from the depths below them, followed by the whine of gears and pulleys bringing the elevator car up to them.

Tensing, the two men took a pace backward, bracing themselves for the possibility of unknown assailants emerging from the door as it slid open... nothing. Having relinquished the flashlight again, Vincent ducked to search every corner, floor to ceiling of the confined space before motioning with his pistol for George to enter. George, complying, wrinkled his nose in revulsion as he walked in and turned to face his partner.

"You weren't kidding... My Lord, the stink."

Vincent allowed the doors to remain open in a fruitless attempt to clear the redolence of revelry from the air as he examined the button console. Five levels were marked, including ENTERTAINMENT at level 4 and GUEST ACCOMMODATION below that. Still, his eyes were drawn to a spot at the bottom of the panel where another button should have been — a smooth patch in the same silvered material as the surrounding panel. He pressed the surface as if it were a button, but to no avail.

"Seen this type of thing before?"

A hand settled on his shoulder as George leaned closer.

"Maybe, I used to deliver to sheltered apartment buildings for Fed-Ex when I worked my after-school job. The fire-marshal showed me how to get past the intercom by pressing the highest and lowest number simultaneously for a whole second. I doubt it'll work here…"

Anticipating George's answer before he'd even finished, Vincent pressed 1 and 5. He held them to the satisfying clatter of the door sliding closed and the lurch of the elevator as it started on its downward journey.

"So Vince," murmured George, picking up his previous probing inquiry, "why do you think there are still Dorians around? They shoulda died ages ago."

Vincent reached gingerly into an inner breast pocket and withdrew a folded polymer sleeve containing a page of lined A4 paper. It was well-worn but had been treated with care despite its age. He handed it to George.

"Here."

The document was hand-written in a way that suggested the writer was competent, but possibly extremely stressed or under duress. In places, the pen appeared to cut deeply into the paper. Some of the commas and periods had almost punctured the page completely. He began scanning efficiently through the text as his police training had taught him. And even as the elevator came to rest with a grinding rattle, Vincent held his finger on the closed-door button until his companion looked up.

CHAPTER 5

For centuries humans have mused, studied, built religions around, and generally agonized over the fate of the soul when the body has expired. The very definition of the soul has been the focus of more than a smattering of adepts. They have philosophized its substance, or lack thereof, its ability to attach itself to a new life, have its time over, or depart the Earth altogether. They surmise whether or not it travels to another dimension, and if so, what kind of place this after-life world might be — one of torment, ecstasy, peace, or conflict... Some even suggest that the soul is a delicate balance of two parts. A physical body comprised of dust (the natural elements like carbon, hydrogen, nitrogen, calcium, etc.). And 'the breath of life' as God had initially breathed into Adam's nostrils at the moment of man's creation. The blood carries this gift, the oxygen, for the duration of life, thus making it a sacred liquid, and when the last breath leaves the body, it ceases to be a soul, and as such, the soul dies.

What, though, if the body has not expired in the strictest sense? What, for example, if the person has been in an accident and after some time been successfully revived? Has their soul departed and then been cruelly yanked back to this imperfect existence?

Or what if the body has been artificially shut down, preserved in a kind of limbo? Like those wealthy individuals who sign expensive contracts to be frozen in cryonic stasis? Do the souls stay, hovering above the chambers like watchful angels waiting for the day of reunification with their host bodies? Or does the soul as the sum of 'dust plus the breath of life' — the raw elements constituting a human body + oxygen stored in the inert tissues — remain dormant, yet undead, within the cryogenic tubes, awaiting reanimation?

Walls of capsules loomed column-like on either side of a morbid, gothic-styled cavern with a roof that could only be seen as a result of the dim violet, red and amber lighting, set pointing upward from hidden recesses in the rock walls. Blinking LEDs betrayed the only evidence of life's potential in the otherwise smooth, black surfaces of each technological coffin. Steam curled lazily from no apparent source and dissipated as it reached the dry upper expanse of the subterranean gallery. At one end of the vast atrium, a vertical slash of light suddenly cut into the cold inky blackness and broadened as the metal door slid aside.

Detectives Cox and Van Helden felt like asthmatics trying to inhale a breath that refused to be drawn as they took in the full magnitude of the scene spread out before them. They stood in stolid silence as they allowed their eyes to adjust and roam the area's length and depth. George was oblivious to the paper dropping from his shaking fingers, and when he finally spoke, it was in a strained voice that Vincent barely recognized.

"Holy Mother; how did you... find out about all this?"

The other man didn't respond immediately, choosing instead to approach the nearest cryogenic tube and start examining the surface systematically with the focused beam of his flashlight. As the light came to rest on the small control panel with the little blue-and-green diodes, he sighed heavily and clicked the handheld light off, plunging them into impenetrable shadow once again. He gestured to George to move to the other side of the corridor and started to explain:

"This investigation goes back about 150 years. It started with one of my ancestors, an actress you may have heard of — Courtney Pippin — who was caught up in the first outbreak of The Dorian Effect and fought long and hard until her death to protect the victims from harm. Sadly, she was able to do little, and the situation exploded way out of her control. First came the social shaming, then the hired private army and security force backlash on the public until the Hollywood fortunes ran out, then the almost overnight ugly turn to mob violence, the police indifference, kidnappings, murders... Then, the reconstitution and decriminalization of both sides, and eventually, the 'cooling-off period.' People simply let their memories of the stigmas fade and move on with their lives. Pockets of gangs would still cause trouble for the Dorians from time to time, and as a group, they rarely traveled alone. They also couldn't find work very efficiently, being relegated to the margins of society and tended to find menial work in janitorial positions, lowly administrative tasks working on their computers from home, or in freak-fest shows. As their generation eventually died out, so did the public interest in them. Until Courtney Pippin stumbled across one of the scariest forms of human traffic ever conceived, and they killed her before she could raise the alarm."

He paused as George called out from a purpose-built glass office nestled amongst the giant cylinders.

"Over here, it's an inventory — written on *paper*."

George sounded incredulous at the concept of such an ancient form of recording, despite reading the page Vince had given him. He held up a metal clipboard and shone the light for them to see. It was a list of names, dates, and an unknown system of grading.

It was the names of over seventy famous Dorian celebrities, each of whom had disappeared and were presumed to have died in the initial conflicts of the first tumultuous years of insanity.

"What? You mean to say they are all *here*?"

"I really wished I was going to be wrong, George, but that page is from one of Courtney's journals I found in the bottom of a cupboard when my family went to sell off the property and settle her estate — what was left of it. She'd long suspected that many of her colleagues were being kidnapped and imprisoned. She spent almost all of her remaining fortune in searching for the answers. Her last journal entry outlined how she feared the worst after multiple thefts of the products used in cryogenics processes and was going to the authorities with the evidence. She was found, as you probably remember, face down in a hotel bath filled with ice-water. The trail has been cold for years, but I believe that's because the masterminds of this atrocity have been sitting on it for years, letting it mature like fifty-year-old scotch whiskey for the right moment to present it to the *sickos* who can afford to sample it."

"Sample it how?"

"As I began to get closer, I heard rumors of orgiastic parties for the super-rich, where unsuspecting guests would be invited and transported with blindfolds and headphones playing loud music so they couldn't give away the location. Once there, they would be exposed to horrific spectacles of caged Dorian victims. The latter successfully defrosted and forced to perform all sorts of menial acts to entertain those watching. The only merciful side-effect is that those revived only lived on for a few months. Of course, this only drives up the price and rarity of these soirees, making it even more difficult to track them."

The two men were suddenly startled by the elevator's sound beginning another ascent and realized that someone must have seen the hole in the wall with the exposed wires and guessed they were on one of the levels.

Vincent regarded George with a suddenly resolute and withering stare. With gradual realization, George felt a chill spread through his shoulders and down his back.

"This was a one-shot deal. Right, Partner?"

He looked down as Vincent drew six small disks from his coat pockets, three in each hand. George instantly recognized them as high-density phosphorus explosives, used primarily in building demolition. Vincent held out his hand to his colleague, proffering a mixed future of complicity, stark mortality, and finality. He uttered a cliché that could only grace the lips of a Hollywood movie star when it had still meant something to be one:

"Let's end this thing once and for all."

THE COUNTRY JAUNT

Author's note - This is not really a story so much as relating a fictitious incident. The circumstances happen all too frequently and are based loosely on real life events from my distant past.

1

Miriama kept one hand fixed firmly on the wheel, her nails digging sharply into the cheap vinyl cover as she wiped the moisture from her face with the back of the other hand. The salty water stung her chapped, sunburnt cheeks and neck and lank wisps of her dyed-chestnut hair clung to her forehead in disarray. The two sources of salt water, however, were very different.

The sweat beaded and trickled from her every pore with irritating regularity in the intense heat of the station-wagon's interior. It mingled its discomfort factor with the odour of four hot, dirty and boisterous children and a ten-week-old puppy. Outside, the sun beat down with ferocity on the brown dry hills and fields, reflecting its intense heat toward the lone vehicle that rattled slowly through the sparse countryside. The car was devoid of air-conditioning, and the heater fan buzzed feebly, almost mockingly, from the cracked dashboard. Stifled, sore, hungry and desperately tired she let the tears continue to brim and burst, forming new channels through the wet grime between her eyes and chin.

Although she had paid some attention to the shrieks, cries and complaints from the rear seat at the outset of the journey, she now found herself in a kind of detached, semiconscious stupor. White painted lines and red-and-white painted posts drifted toward her with monotonous regularity. She stayed between them only out of habit. The two older children had begun to entertain themselves by finding things to throw out onto the road behind them. The two younger ones had taken to eating whatever interesting small items they came across in the cluttered boot space, whether it was of human origin or not. The puppy had joined in this activity and, from time to time, contributed by occasionally producing that-*which-was-not*.

The car had been on the road since 2:45 am that morning. Her husband's habitual drunken, drug-taking behaviour had resulted in yet another painful beating. It might have been more severe had he not been momentarily distracted by a flashing light somewhere outside and stood up suddenly from where he was standing over her. He'd caught his head on the sharp corner of an open cupboard door and knocked himself out cold. Crawling out from under his fifteen stone unconscious weight, she'd used the extension cord from the refrigerator and tied his wrist to the drainage pipe under the sink.

Finally, nursing her bruised (and possibly cracked) ribs, she had simply emptied the drawers from each room into canvas carry bags and thrown them, along with blankets and linen, into the back of the rusting Kingswood station wagon. Her nearest relative – her older brother Tamati – lived nearly thirteen hours away, in Takaka. Emptying her inert husband's pockets and the hidden jar where she kept fifty or sixty dollars for food, (just in case he spent all of his wages on beer and drugs, which frequently happened) she had loaded the kids and dog into the car and left.

Surprisingly, the tank had been three-quarters full, and she had filled it twice since. It was now 11:30. The car had been on the road non-stop, for almost nine hours. The best speed she could get from the spluttering, misfiring old heap, was eighty-five kilometres an hour. They were barely even two-thirds of the way to Takaka, and the money was all gone.

Yet still – she drove.

⌘

The engine noise had deteriorated, and the petrol light had been on for twenty minutes when Miriama limped into the small, barely noticeable town of Ward.

The petrol station was right next to the tearooms, and the Kingswood came to rest in the gravel between them. Despite knowing that there was not a drop of fuel in the tank, she tried turning the engine over several times, hoping to move forward to a less conspicuous parking space. Finally, through a fresh stream of tears and vulgarity, she threw up her hands in desperation, buried her face in her arms over the steering wheel, and cried with great shuddering sobs.

For the first time since they had set out from Greenhills so many hours ago, the children fell quiet. Climbing into the front bench-seat next to her, Wikitoria, her eldest, put a comforting arm about her mother's shoulders, "Don't be sad, Mum," she said. Pausing, she continued: "Can we have some food now... please?"

The simple platitudes of her innocent offspring snapped Miriama back to reality.

Miriama wiped her face on a dirty towel from the floor in front of the passenger's seat. She looked around to survey the damage that children and dog had inflicted on the rear of the car. Instinctively taking a breath to angrily berate them she checked herself, realising just what they had been through and endured since the day before.

"I'm going to go inside and see if I can get some lunch from the nice people in the shop, kids, so just behave for a few minutes – OK?" She summoned her most convincing smile and climbed out before any of them could think of a complaint to hit her with.

A light jingling echoed around the interior of the small shop from a bell attached to the top corner of the door and as she entered she was greeted with the sweet smell of iced cakes, mince pies and coffee. For the first time since getting into the car that morning, she realised from the sudden rush of saliva in her mouth just how empty her stomach was. She opened her purse and looked with trepidation into it to see if she could afford to buy anything. There were three coins: a fifty, a twenty and a five – seventy-five cents. Her shoulders sagged, and she felt dizzy. Swaying, she moved to an empty table and sat down.

Feeling the gentle pressure of a small hand on her shoulder, she turned to see Wikitoria looking with childish innocence into her eyes.

"There's not enough, eh, Mum?" she said. "Why don't you ring Uncle T to come and get us? He's got lots of money, hasn't he?"

Pulling out the seat next to her, Miriama smiled and said: "Come sit here Bub, I don't know what I'd do without you. I'll see if the shopkeeper will let me ring your uncle."

Approaching the counter, she waited until the harried-looking owner emerged from the back room. Perhaps it hasn't been his day either, she thought to herself as she looked at his glowing forehead and cheeks. The oven-cloth slung over one shoulder completed the picture of a man with more than a few jobs on the go at one time.

"Can I help you?" he said gruffly.

"I... I was hoping you might let me use your telephone. My car desperately needs attention, and I have to ring my brother for help... if you don't mind?" As she added the last part, she blinked a stray tear away that had been forming and sniffed quietly.

Forcing air between his slightly pursed lips in a kind of peeved sigh, he then asked: "Got money for the toll call?"

"Oh, don't worry, I'll call collect." Noticing that this statement hadn't impressed him, she continued: "You can dial the operator yourself if you like."

After a moment of silence, he twisted one side of his mouth up in a sort of sneer and shook his head. Lifting one side of the counter, he motioned for her to follow him to where the phone sat, on a small wall shelf. Sitting next to it, also on the shelf, was a small tear-off notepad – and a pencil.

She quickly dialled and gave the operator her brother's residential details, asking for a collect called to be placed to that number. When he finally picked up and accepted the charges, she broke down and told him the whole miserable story. Once he'd calmed her down again, Tamati told her to give him the number for the store she was ringing from and said he would ring back shortly, once he'd made some arrangements.

Passing this information on to the shopkeeper, who had occupied himself with taking empty cardboard boxes out to the skip; she then slumped down onto the wicker chair beside the telephone to wait.

Meanwhile, at the other end of the phone, her brother Tamati hung up and quickly dialled the number for his friend George. He'd been friendly with George for years – ever since they'd worked in the freezing industry together during the eighties. Even though Tamati had moved from Blenheim to live in Takaka with his new wife, he'd never stopped ringing his mate every couple of months and sending the odd lewd postcard.

2

George Watene was one of the smartest men on his block. His reputation was such that people came even from the next town to ask him to solve problems for them. It made him feel good to be so highly sought after, and he prided himself on his ability to use his brain instead of abuse it – like ninety per cent of his neighbours. By the time he'd hung up the phone and grabbed his coat, a plan was forming. He quickly drove through downtown Blenheim and drew up outside 'The Marlborough Lawyers and Associated Legal Services Centre.'

He went inside for about thirty seconds – came out and used his mobile phone to dial the phone number his friend had given him for the diner. When Miriama answered, he explained that he was a very close friend of her brother and that he would take care of everything. He then asked:

"Have you told him who your brother is, or what he does for a living?"

When she replied in the negative, he told her to put the owner on the phone. Presently a gruff voice at the other end said: "Who's this?"

"My name is Dr Rewi Porter, and I manage the Marlborough Lawyers Association in Blenheim. I understand that my sister and her children have broken down at your café, is that correct?"

"Yeah, that's right – and they don't have any money either."

"Are you familiar with the Legal Service Centre in town, Mr-?"

"Webb; yeah, I think I know the one you mean. Why?"

"Because I want you to hang up the phone, look up our number in your phone book and ring me back here, so you know that I'm telling you the truth. If you do that, I'll make it worth your while."

After a strained pause, the man sighed heavily, mumbled something unintelligibly affirmative and hung up the phone.

Quickly George went into the reception area again and approached the girl behind the richly carved, very expensive looking mahogany counter.

Waving a small pill bottle in her direction, he said with an air of urgency: "Can you get me a bunch of paper towels and a cup of warm water for my wife, please? We're from 'out of town', and she's been having quite severe heart problems. That would really help."

The receptionist blinked at him a few times, as if to say, you're interrupting something important here but, as he'd guessed, she couldn't ignore his request. Carefully hiding the combination she was punching in, she disappeared through the large door behind her chair. It clicked shut behind her.

A moment later, the telephone on her desk rang.

Affecting the most sickly, lisping effeminate voice he could muster, he answered with: "Legal Services, Marlborough – how may I help you?"
"Yeah, this is Gordon Webb, from the Ward Diner. Mr Porter's expecting a call from me."

"Just one moment, please... Dr Porter, a call for you from a Mr Gordon Webb, is that OK? You'll call him back on the mobile? Yes, I'll let him know. Mr Webb? Mr Porter is on his way out to the car, and he's calling you on his mobile phone right now."

He hung up the phone just as the receptionist returned with a plastic cup of water. She handed him the cup and small sealed packet of tissues. He thanked her and hurried outside, tossing them into a rubbish bin as he hit the redial button.

The irritated café owner picked up again.

"Yeah?"

"Mr Webb, what I want you to do is quite simple. One: give my sister and the children some lunch and, if you've got the facilities, a shower. Two: fill her car with petrol and check the oil and water for her. I will arrive after the conclusion of my working day and pay all expenses incurred plus an additional five hundred dollars. Is that arrangement satisfactory to you?"

Gordon Webb had been about to complain about how he wasn't a charity and didn't owe those people anything when he heard the mention of the extra half grand.

"Ah… um…" he coughed, "yeah, that should be OK, I suppose."

"Very good. Can you put my sister back on the phone please, Mr Webb."

With a slightly glazed look in his eyes, Gordon handed the receiver back to Miriama.

"Sis, you gotta listen to me real careful OK?" George said. Without waiting for an answer, he continued, firing instructions at her so that she didn't have time to argue their morality. To keep up, she simply had to mechanically follow them, one after another.

"Is the phonebook still opened to the Lawyer's office? Good. Tear that page out and put it in your pocket." Miriama did so, folding the page into a small square and stuffing it into her brassiere. It was at this moment she realised that the number was also scrawled on the notepad. She told George.

"OK, tear off a few pages, we don't want anyone taking a rubbing for the next day or so. Have you done that? Good. Now, can the owner see you, where you are? Well, hide the phonebook somewhere under a cabinet or a couch so he won't find it straight away. Done. All right, go out to the diner and give those kids a good feed and a shower. Don't worry, I'm paying for it. I've told the owner to look after you well, so you just take what you need and get going to Takaka, OK? Good. Take care now, little sister."

With that, he hung up.

Forty minutes later, the decrepit Kingswood once again swung onto State Highway 1; somewhat quieter now, with a fresh crankcase of oil and a tank full of premium petrol. Even so, as the bedraggled vehicle pulled away, it still managed a smoke-laden splutter of protest.

Staring after it, Gordon Webb shook his head, squinting as the late afternoon sun glanced off the back window of the shrinking car. He glanced at his watch – almost five-thirty. It wouldn't be long now.

THE CRYPTOGRAPHER'S INK

Based on an idea by Cristina Douglas

CHAPTER ONE — 2019

The mixed aromas of stale coffee and cigarettes never dissipated from the cramped staffroom of The Hannerton Rest Home and Hospice Service. Of course, the facility was non-smoking, but it didn't take long for the exhaled breath and discarded coats of men and women returning from the frozen exile of the lone smoking shelter outside to infiltrate the furniture and wallpaper.

Rose Pickett, 31, wasn't one of the smokers, although to be fair, she struggled from time to time with relapses when stress levels got too high. It wasn't hard to flounder in this place with frequent periods of understaffing, budget cuts and the seasonal infections that swept through the home.

She'd read that something like a third of the population of Europe had been wiped out during the black plague, a statistic grimly reflected at times in the numbers of residents whose weakened immune systems failed to cope when struck by gastroenteritis, or worse, a localised flu. It only took one individual to return from an excursion with a bit of a sniffle, and the effects could be horrendous.

Anyway, the health of residents in recent months had been fair (touch wood), the weather was warming up, and for the moment there seemed to be enough staff numbers to make life manageable and relatively stress-free. There was only one potential stress point in the day — handover.

She hung her jacket in a locker, smoothed out her uniform, attached a magnetic name badge and headed for the staff room.

Her colleague, Margaret Boyce, was still sitting at the shared computer workstation typing up a report when Rose entered. She felt a twinge of concern immediately, as reports usually meant incidents, which generally involved extra monitoring or emergency strategy plans.

With a nervous sing-song voice, she piped up:

"Uh-oh… this doesn't look too promising, Maggie. How's your night been?"

The much older woman replied in a somewhat gravelly tone that belied her gentle nature:

"Not so bad, sweetheart — just a bit *weirder* than your usual Thursday night."

"Yeah?"

"Yeah, must be something in the air conditioning or the food — who knows."

Rose didn't say anything, allowing space for her colleague to elaborate in her own good time. She reached for her coffee mug, hanging from the row of hooks over the sink and opened the little bar fridge to find some milk. As she did so, Margaret finished typing, saved her work and swivelled the office chair to address Rose more directly.

"Ted Campbell; how has he seemed to you the last couple of weeks — I mean, what's his typical day looking like?"

Rose had just switched on the kettle and moved to sit in a dining chair at the lunch table. She pursed her lips in thought and replied:

"No different from usual, I'd say… Ted pretty much followed the same routine last week as he has since I've known him. He's awake in the mornings when I come in to help him dress for breakfast and tends not to swerve too much from his menu choices: eggs on toast, or cereal.

"Reads the paper in the day-room for an hour 'til I've found someone to help me give him his shower and usually by the time we're done, his friend Wally is waiting for him in reception. They sit and chat to the ladies in the day room for a while and Wally brings a packed lunch and eats with Ted. Then they go to Ted's room for some private 'guy talk' for a couple of hours and then Wally usually leaves, and Ted rests for a wee while.

"I wake him up for a cup of tea around fourish, and we chat for a while if there's time before the evening meal. He goes to bed early and falls asleep listening to the BBC, and I usually come in about 9 to turn the radio off."

"So, no signs of anxiety or stress that you've noticed?"

Rose frowned. She was quite fond of old Ted, who'd been at the rest home for quite a few years before she'd taken up a position as a care worker. Ted was ninety, suffered from dementia, but was courteous and polite and had been a gentleman, and a very gentle man, in his younger days.

"What sort of things? I mean sure, he gets easily confused when his dementia is more prominent, like when he's ill or a bit run down, but then he responds pretty quickly to someone talking to him and calming him down."

As an afterthought, she added:

"I haven't done the night-shift for about three weeks though — has he been different?"

"He's been acting up a bit lately, which is totally out of character for him, but we can't put the finger on a cause or trigger at the moment." Margaret shifted her weight in the chair and continued: "He's been coming out of his room around eight o'clock and wandering, looking lost and a bit frightened when people approach him. And he seems to shrink back when people reach out to help him or guide him back to his room. If I didn't know better, I'd think he was sleepwalking, but he seems to be wide awake."

Rose sighed, feeling a little deflated at the news.

"Oh, dear, that's a bit of a worry," she muttered.

She always hated the part when residents experienced or exhibited change. It could mean nothing, or it could be the beginning of the end — sometimes a disconcertingly swift end. Compassion fatigue was a frequent and silent assailant in the care profession, and it was all that most nurses and care-workers could do to bury their personal feelings and start each shift like it was just another day.

"I'll try to get a lucid moment with him today to see if he'll talk about it," she said.

She stood, turning away from Margaret to hide a lumpy swallow and moved to switch the cooling kettle back on.

CHAPTER TWO – 2006

Wallace 'Wally' Northam told the taxi driver to pull over. He produced his leather wallet and asked what price he owed for the trip. The driver looked at the elderly passenger in the mirror a little perplexedly and asked if this was the right address. Wishing to retain an air of mystery by never giving the correct address, Wally merely replied that he could make his way from here.

His lifelong friend and ex-army compadre, Edward 'Ted' Campbell had indicated on the phone that he wanted to meet quite urgently, so Wally had called his housekeeper and told her to take the weekend off. He then caught the lunchtime train up from his home in Cheltenham.

Ted hadn't sounded worried so much as perturbed and Wally half-expected that there was some scientific or possibly ecological conundrum that Ted wanted help solving. They had a 'sounding board' relationship that neither of their late wives had appreciated much. This, however, had been tolerated as a concession to the ladies' lack of understanding of all things 'war'. Both men had married girls much younger than themselves who had grown up in a world more than a decade removed from that dreadful conflict.

Once the taxi was out of sight, Wally merely crossed the road and rang the doorbell at the ground floor entrance to one of two semi-detached houses. Ted, still slender of build and not quite six feet tall, arrived and greeted his visitor with a warm handshake. He led him to a conservatory overlooking the typically sparse patch of garden that most terraced homes in English suburbs boasted. Wally patiently followed his shuffling host through the house and lowered himself into a comfortable outdoor wicker settee.

His companion poured him a single malt with ice but did not sit straight away, preferring to stand looking at the overcast vista outdoors. Momentarily he appeared to shrug off his malaise and turned to gesture toward an opened envelope and letter laying unfolded on his oak coffee table.

"I've been seeing a specialist and having quite a few tests over the last couple of months," he began, "I was hoping that they were mistaken but, unfortunately..."

The two had known each other too long for Wally to let his mouth fall open, aghast in *faux* shock and concern. Instead, he merely took up the thread of conversation with his characteristic warmth.

"Well, better to know for sure than be stuck wondering, right?"

Ted raised his eyebrows, tilted his head in assent and sat down in the chair opposite. He wasn't in the habit of mincing words.

"Early signs of dementia — not particularly aggressive, but still marching toward the inevitable *memory turning into a forgettory*."

He paused to sip his drink and sat back into the chair cushions; his gaze seemingly drawn again to the muted grey exterior.

"Anyway, I've had time to do a lot of reading and thinking on the subject, and a few things stick out that you might be able to help me with."

Wally shook his glass gently, allowing the remnants of ice to clink gently against the sides. His willingness and preparedness to help his friend went without saying, but etiquette warranted a moment to let the gravity of the situation settle upon the room.

"I'm sorry to hear that, chum, truly I am. What sorts of things can I help with?"

Ted extracted a lined notepad from the gap between the seat cushion and the arm of his chair and handed it across the table to Wally. The top page was about three-quarters filled with spidery hand-written squiggles. This simplistic shorthand was a code that both men had used successfully during the second world war. While they had been forced to go back to using the standard Roman alphabet after the war, Ted had opted only to do this for official papers and letters to people. All other writing, he did in this efficient artificial language that he and Wally had invented between them. As the other man scanned through the page, Ted explained:

"It seems pretty important to keep practising my good habits, so they stick even when I don't know who I am."

Wally nodded:

"Like muscle memory, I guess."

Ted licked his lips and went on:

"You're the only one who knows everything about me; you can help me remember. Some things help in the later stages... so they say."

Wally looked up from the pad.

"Things like what?" he asked.

"Playing familiar music, pictures of family and stuff. Some hospitals and rest homes even keep dogs and cats."

Wally opened his mouth to speak, but his friend held up his hand and went on:

"Wal, I don't want to die, but I don't want to end up a burden to my friends and family either. Not knowing them or myself or having any hint of the person I used to be."

Ted wasn't an overtly emotional man, nor was he given to displays of anger or high anxiety, but Wally did notice a glassiness forming in his friend's eyes.

Smiling and shaking his head, Wally ran his finger down the page as he mused aloud:

"It says here… where is it? Ah, this part about *visual cues*, like you said, pictures and such."

"Yep?"

"Hmmm."

Wally stroked his chin and took off his reading spectacles. He blinked a few times and appeared to be rooted in thought. After a few minutes of silence, he picked up his glass and downed the remaining liquid. A wry grin slowly started to form at the sides of his mouth.

He said, in a mysterious voice:

"You know Edward, I'm beginning to get just an inkling of how we could do this."

Ted's fingers were steepled in concentration as he regarded Wally from across the oak coffee table in his conservatory.

"And what inkling is that pray tell?" he asked, casually.

"You and I still are part of one of the largest secret communities in the world, even though it disappeared after the war, right?"

As he posed this question, Wally flitted his eyes suggestively toward the whisky bottle on the sideboard, and Ted nodded. Wally stood and gathered both glasses to be re-charged while his friend leaned forward and took back the writing pad, setting it on his knee and taking a pen from the breast pocket of his brushed-cotton shirt.

Mention of the war was causing Ted to experience a fleeting flashback to the moment when he realised that Wally had, in an unprecedented act of kindness, dragged him from the brink of hell at the Italian front. It had been a kind act shown to an injured man he had met just days before.

CHAPTER THREE — 2019

The regular handover notes regarding long-time resident, Mr Ted Campbell, indicated that, while not intensifying significantly, his episodes of wandering from his room and trying in a state of confusion to escape the safe confines of the rest home complex had not abated.

Now that Rose Pickett's shift pattern had once again switched over to nights, she was able to observe first-hand the curious behaviour he had recently developed. Mercifully, he didn't seem to have had any decline in physical health, and his appetite remained unaffected. However, the regular night walks seemed to be here to stay.

Rose felt more concerned over the effect that attempting to intervene seemed to have on Ted Campbell when he was in the middle of one of these excursions. Usually a jovial and soft-mannered gentleman with a helpful and empathetic outlook, he seemed utterly out-of-sorts — wide-eyed, anxious and easily frightened if startled from behind. Another uncharacteristic facet of this new behaviour was to whisper to himself in an almost reproachful tone as if telling himself off for forgetting something vital.

It was 11:30 PM now, and Ted Campbell was back in bed sleeping, the registered nurse had finished her night round, and it was an opportunity to use the quiet time to get as much administrative work done as possible. Rose checked the ward thermostat to ensure that nobody would get too hot and throw their blankets off during the night. Now that the weather had improved, it was ironic how many residents managed to give themselves a chill this way.

She made her way to the staff office. Two of the newer care workers were already there, sharing the newspaper and drinking tea. Thea was 19 years old with very light brown, almost blonde hair and rather unfortunate, uneven skin as a vestige of acne from her teen years. She looked up and volunteered a small smile.

"You want tea, Rosie? There's still a couple of cups left in the pot."

"Thanks, yeah, I'll get some. All the rounds finished? No emergencies to report?"

Maria, the other girl, looked up from the paper and spoke in a slightly husky tone. She had quite a strong accent, and Rose sometimes felt a little embarrassed at asking her to repeat herself. Maria tended to be quite popular among the male residents, not in any inappropriate way, but seemed at ease with them and found that joking with them came very naturally. She had jet black hair and very dark features.

"I think Mister Ted was much more agitated tonight. He didn't want me to come near him, and it is the first time that I hear him shouting at me."

Rose frowned, feeling a little alarmed, but keeping her emotions to herself. Although she'd checked on Ted later in the evening, she had not personally been present during tonight's incident. As she sat down in the computer chair and tapped the space bar to let the machine warm up, she asked:

"When he shouted, did he say anything different from what he usually mumbles?"

Maria looked over at Thea, as they had both helped Ted through the ordeal, eventually leading him back to his room. Thea swallowed the rest of her mouthful of biscuit and replied:

"It was different, yeah. Normally Ted only talks to himself and puts himself down, but today he raised his voice at us directly.

He said: 'No, don't, I'm not going back, please don't make me,' and when we eventually managed to take his arms and start leading him back, he sounded almost like he'd given up and said: 'I'm not going to do it again.' He said that a couple of times."

Rose listened, mystified, and all she could think to say was:

"That poor man, what on Earth is going on in that mind of his?"

Maria had turned back to the paper but answered off-handedly:

"Mister Ted is afraid of us taking him away."

"Yeah, but we haven't said anything about taking him any-where!" interjected Thea. "I tried to say to him that this is his home and he's not going away, but I'm not convinced he even knows where he is during these episodes, he's so frantic and pan-icky all the time."

Thea looked across at Rose and added:

"Remember how the only thing that seemed to calm him down was showering him? Once he'd finished drying and combing his hair in the mirror, he would instantly be gentle as a lamb again."

Rose nodded, having used this method many times to help put Ted in a calm mood, especially when his dementia was making him feel more confused than usual. Thea went on:

"Not anymore — I tried it tonight, he got to the point of being so upset he started crying. It just didn't work."

Maria again chimed in with an apparently unrelated comment, not looking up from the paper:

"Mister Ted likes to look at his tattoos."

Rose felt a smile creeping across her face. Maria didn't say much, but she certainly wasn't slow or stupid. She agreed thoroughly that Ted's tattoos seemed to give him great pleasure and were a significant catalyst in reducing anxiety. This was often the case with dementia patients that a familiar photo, picture, song or tune tended to calm them and induce serenity. She said, half to herself as her mind drifted:

"Yes – those bloody tattoos."

"I don't even think he can read them," said Thea, "it doesn't even look like a real language — just symbols and squiggly lines."

"I think he can," said Rose, "I asked him once, and he said he learned this language on a hill in India, during the second world war. I've never asked him what they said — it always felt a bit rude somehow."

She glanced at her watch and turned to type her password into the computer.

"It is a bit of a worry if even *that* isn't working to de-escalate him anymore. We'll have to report this to the psych support team in case there is an underlying medical issue that Ted has recently developed."

CHAPTER FOUR — 1943

The White Hart Public House in Drury Lane, London had been an established landmark since 1216. Frequented by many a famous and infamous face throughout its history, it was at one time known as a regular stop for condemned men to have a final drink and 'the comforts of a woman' before marching on to the gallows.

Fortuitously unaffected by the shaking and crumbling of the war going on around it, the pub had also become a final stepping off place for innocent young men to go and turn forever into scarred soldiers of war. Thus it was, in early 1943, when a group of six young men who'd arrived from various locales across lower England met to toast the receiving of their war assignments before reporting the next day for duty. They each possessed — more or less official — papers confirming the reaching of legal age and arrived with a mixture of reluctance and anticipation.

Dennis Oakley, Peter Mulley, Edward Campbell, Wilfred Noel-Baker, Christopher Perry and Jack Caruthers sat on benches, three-on-a-side, at a long table under a dusty stag's head that had eyes staring vacantly in different directions. Each was taking it, in turn, to mention a father or brother already actively stationed somewhere and telling the others where he'd either been assigned already or soon hoped to be. Mulley and Noel-Baker, fresh from a collegiate crash course in first aid, were bound for a medical frigate where they'd been assigned as junior medics. Christopher Perry, broad and powerfully built, fully expected to follow in his older brother's footsteps and be sent to train as a paratrooper. He boasted about the hundreds of kills his brother had made but wasn't much able to cite his information sources when pressed.

Campbell, although quiet most of the time, had come across to the rest as something of a nervous philosopher, merely interjecting now and then with questions about hypothetical combat scenarios. He asked if faced with an unarmed German soldier of similar age, looking scared and not the slightest bit confrontational, would they choose to kill the man on the spot? Would they instead use it as an opportunity to draw attention to the commonalities they shared, trying to force a bond of some sort? Dennis Oakley, red-faced and rather bad-tempered, consistently shot these statements down with cries of 'that sort of talk is treason' and 'only good Jerry is a dead Jerry' followed by a call to toast his profound claims.

As each member of the group slowly meandered off to meet their destinies, Campbell found himself seated with Jack Caruthers — the only remaining individual at the table. Caruthers casually fished out a cigarette and offered the pack to Edward who gratefully accepted. The two men smoked in silence, and after a minute or so, Caruthers spoke.

"I sensed strong misgivings from you this evening, although it hardly seemed the appropriate place and time for you to make a stand," he said with an air of pretentiousness. "For the last four years, I've watched droves of Britain's finest — and anyone else they can lay hands on — marching off, chests bursting with patriotic fervour and inculcated blood-lust."

Campbell remained silent, nodding with uncertainty as his companion went on, wondering at where this conversation might be leading.

"What Hitler is doing to people in his own country, just because of their religious and racial background is atrocious, and he deserves to die thousands of times over, but I'm sure there could have been a more covert way of doing it. Or maybe there isn't."

Staring at his drink, Campbell seemed to be searching for answers in its murky depths.

"I... don't know how I feel, or what I want. I just know that I don't have what it takes to kill another person, whatever the reason."

"Campbell, isn't it? Campbell, you won't get far in this Man's Army with that attitude. They'll assume you're some sort of weakling or fairy, or worst of all, a coward. Mark my words: you'll be shot for that in a heartbeat once they find out. You need to find something to do that won't singe your conscience too much. You still have to be an active contributor to the war effort."

Edward Campbell looked up, dejectedly.

"I'm not terribly good at anything. Since school, I've only worked part-time as a runner for the local paper. I hoped to keep in their good graces long enough to step up as a copywriter one day. I've no experience in engineering or nursing or administration. As far as the army is concerned, I'm only good for carrying a gun and shooting the enemy."

"I'm sure they need newspapermen to report from the frontlines, but I doubt they'll consider a runner as being adequately qualified for the task. What did you do in school — did you get good grades?"

Edward sighed, shaking his head.

"I got high marks, but I never took any practical, tactile subjects. I did history, geography, languages — that sort of thing."

Caruthers finished his cigarette and prepared to leave.

"I'd like to be more encouraging, but to be honest, I think you've got a helluva tough road ahead. The army's no place for lightweights, but if it's any consolation, every hardened soldier in the Great War was a lightweight going in. Maybe it'll be just what you need."

Campbell felt the words grip him as he watched the other man pay his bar bill and then march out into the chilled, smoky London evening.

⌘

The smoothness and relative calm of the flight gave a false sense of security to the motley crew of boys, barely out of school most of them and utterly unprepared for the carnage that lay ahead. The aeroplane doors swung open upon the unforgiving inferno of North Africa, and they spent several weeks of gruelling drills to learn to trust their rifle as their best and only friend. During this time Edward Campbell suffered various bouts of rising panic, intertwined with an overwhelming sense of emotional numbness as if his brain were deliberating shutting down his conscience against the prospect of what might happen next.

It was the first week of September, and they boarded Royal Navy vessels, crossing to the south-east shores of Italy, arriving eventually at the port of Taranto. United States President Eisenhower had planned this secret landing operation to take advantage of an offer by a now surrendered and beleaguered Italian government. The inroads to the country were steadily being cleared by troops that had parachuted in earlier. However, they still encountered resistance from their German counterparts in the form of ambushes and skirmishes along the way.

Edward marched with his group three days and nights, through harsh winds that dried his eyes and cracked the skin around his mouth. The unsympathetic officers in charge spurred the men on, sneering at their minor irritations and knowing that soon enough they'd be begging for the simple discomfort of chapped lips.

On the afternoon of the fourth day, they arrived at their destination — a strategic position overlooking a recently constructed hydro-electric dam close to the front. While intel was correct that the enemy had left the stronghold to bolster another valley, they were unaware that a small team of enemy soldiers remained behind to guard the dam.

Trudging down the embankment toward the dam buildings, Edward and his comrades were surprised by a grenade explosion and a massive eruption of machine-gun fire. Seven men were killed outright, and five fell wounded in the dirt as the confused and disoriented group dispersed in all directions, seeking shelter wherever it could be found.

As he ran, Edward's heart pounded like a jackhammer, and his breath came in short, stunted gasps. He stumbled upon one of his fellows whose foot had been pulverised by a machine-gun bullet. Swallowing the rising gall in his throat, he hastily tied his canteen strap around the man's calf as a tourniquet and, crouching low, dragged him fifteen feet to an outcrop.

He acted like an automaton, following the relay of commands to retreat with the injured and regroup. The remaining members of the unit then backtracked about half a mile and came around to lower ground through the adjacent forest woodland, using the trees for cover.

A command was issued to start shooting at the windows and doors of the buildings. The grenadiers tried to lob their deadly missiles through any visible openings. Stray bullets whizzed and sang across the battle zone at regular intervals throwing up geysers of dirt and splintering tree-bark, which cut into Edward's skin and threatened to blind him. He cowered in the little depression he had found for shelter — firing his rifle high into the air in the general direction of the river.

Burning foliage and a thick pall of grey smoke stung his eyes and made visibility poor. He could no longer tell which direction the angry shouting of senior officers came from and the muscles of his entire body quivered uncontrollably. Letting go of his rifle, he clasped his ears tightly and buried his face in his arms, curling into a tight foetal ball.

Without warning, a colossal explosion erupted from the direction of the dam and moments later Edward Campbell felt the ground beneath him fall away as if it had been turned to fine dust. Before he lapsed into unconsciousness, a searing heat seemed to engulf him, and he was vaguely aware of the smell of cooking meat… then nothing.

CHAPTER FIVE — 2019

"Thank you all for coming today, I know some have travelled quite some distance to attend."

The Hannerton Rest Home administrator wore a lab coat over his crisply ironed cotton shirt and muted tie. His dark grey trousers were razor-creased, and his pointed brogues shone. Although overseeing a crucial and somewhat sombre proceeding, he managed to inject the right tone of warmth and empathy into his salutation. The group he addressed sat in a well-lit meeting room around a large table. A coffee machine gurgled quietly against one wall at the far end, next to the internal doorway.

He regarded the subject of the gathering, who sat at the conference table in comfortable slacks, polo shirt and sweater, with a blanket across the back of his chair in case he needed it.

"And how are *you* feeling today, Ted?"

Ted Campbell smiled easily and responded evenly:

"I'm fine, thank you. How are you?"

"I'm well, Ted — very well — and thank you for asking. Do you know why we've asked you to come today?"

Ted glanced momentarily at Rose Pickett, and then across the table at his friend Wally. Both smiled warmly at him. He turned again to the front of the room and shook his head.

"Well, it seems that you've been waking up late at night and taking some little excursions around the home. We thought it best to check and make sure you didn't hurt yourself in the process.

Does this make sense?"

Ted nodded, although, to those looking on, he didn't appear to be completely understanding of the whole situation. He waved his hand with a dismissive gesture and said:

"It's all very kind of you, but, totally, unnecessary. I'm not hurt in the slightest."

This last comment was added as something of an afterthought, and Ted seemed visibly embarrassed that he may have made people travel for no reason.

"Not at all, Ted, don't worry, it's an opportunity to give you a good health check-up anyway, and I'm sure everyone is happy to have the opportunity to spend time together."

A murmur of agreement rippled around the table.

"In that case, let's get started. The lovely lady sitting next to you is Doctor Joanne Gainsborough. She's a specialist from London who would like to check if you've got any bruises you haven't noticed, and she will check at the same time if you've had maybe any changes in skin texture or new spots appear that we should be concerned about. Like I said, we'll cover all the bases while we're here. If you'd like to pop behind the screen over there and Ms Pickett can help you put on the gown."

While the administrator was still talking, Rose and the lady doctor had moved to either side of Ted. They helped him stand and walk behind the loose plastic curtain, which housed a basic clinic bed and a table with an assortment of instruments, swabs and ointments. Ted turned as he reached the curtain and, addressing no-one in particular, said:

"Would anyone like a cup of tea while they wait?"

A well-dressed, middle-aged woman who had been sitting quietly immediately spoke up.

"Oh, Dad, bless your heart! Don't worry about us, I'll get a drink for everyone."

Mallory Bertenshaw had been wrapped up, despite the warm weather, but now shed her coat and scarf to go to the coffee dispenser. She wore a Harris Tweed jacket and skirt combination and kept her long hair in a tight bun. She no longer coloured her hair, but her smooth complexion gave her a striking appearance that belied her age.

She was the only daughter of Edward and Edith Campbell and had never had children of her own, choosing instead to focus on her career as an aviation engineer. Her mother had died from cancer at the turn of the millennium, leaving her as her father's only surviving relative. She loved him dearly but had not coped well with his progressive dementia. She visited only intermittently and when requested by the rest home.

After Ted Campbell had been examined and allowed to return, the rest home staff adjourned for a private meeting. The small remaining group found themselves waiting once again at the rather empty boardroom table.

A further 25 minutes and Rose and the other carers returned from the private meeting looking rather upset and distressed. As they sat, two uniformed security men entered the room and stood against the wall quietly. This altered the mood of those present, and consequently, they all looked worriedly at the administrator. He drew a breath and looked up from his notes.

"I'll say first that Mr Campbell does not appear to have suffered an injury as a result of his evening-time incidents and staff-members can be commended for having managed this behaviour appropriately."

He seemed to do a sweep of the guests with his eyes during this pause before resuming:

"However, we have grave concerns about another issue involving Mr Campbell's care. Dr Gainsborough has noted, regarding his tattoos, that from his chest to his lower torso, his tattoos get newer and newer. Of greater concern, is that the most recent tattooing appears to have taken place possibly as recently as two or three months ago."

Quiet gasps could be heard from around the table, and Rose sniffed, dabbing at her eyes with a tissue, feeling irresponsible for not having noticed something wrong with a resident in her care.

"We're not blaming the carers at this time, it was unlikely to be noticed by the untrained eye, but it appears that this inking has been occurring on the premises. Does anyone have information that can shed some light on this... phenomenon?"

A throat cleared, and all eyes were drawn to one seat and two hands, deftly cleaning a pair of reading spectacles.

Wallace Northam continued to clean his glasses, but said in a broken voice:

"I... have that information."

"Mr Northam?"

"I've been tattooing Ted, on and off, since 1943, when we first went to war together. Sometimes with decades in between, but they add up, I guess."

He looked up at the administrator with wide eyes, as if to say, so what?

"Well, I don't like to be the deliverer of unpleasant news, Mr Northam, but what you've been doing is highly illegal. You can't — even consensually — visit and perform activities that expose a person to high risk of infection in an environment that is not remotely safe for you to do so. I gather you've never sought permission from the home to engage in this activity?"

Having spent the best part of half an hour in private conference with the rest home care staff, he already knew the answer to this question but appeared to be dignifying the elderly man with a chance to clear his conscience.

Wally, somewhat chastened, lowered his eyes.

"No, no, we haven't."

The administrator appeared to be struggling with the burden of his pronouncement, but he continued to deliver it anyway.

"Well, since no adverse effect is experienced by Mr Campbell and given your close relationship, we feel that prosecution in this instance is not warranted. Mr Northam, it gives me no pleasure to say this to you, but in future, all visits to the rest home must be fully supervised. Further: for the next 72 hours, until this agreement can be drafted ready for you to sign, you are requested to leave the premises immediately."

Now, with the colour drained from his features, Wally slowly stood facing his friend. His hands shook, and he seemed suddenly even older and frailer than his 90 years.

"I'm sorry, Ted, truly I am," he whispered, realising to himself that he was almost echoing word for word what he had said when Ted first disclosed his dementia diagnosis.

As the two security personnel roused themselves to approach, Rose Pickett stood and waved them back, keeping her hand down by her waist. She walked to Wally's side and helped him with his hat and coat.

"Come on, Wal," she said quietly, "I'll walk you out."

Outside, in the car park, they stopped at the yellow-painted section of roadway where taxis could pick-up or drop off passengers. He looked at Rose with eyes that darted back and forward, searching her face.

"Kate-"

"Rose."

"Rose, yes, sorry. Rose, I need your help. You care about Ted, don't you?"

"Of course, Wally, you know that."

"Then, help me, please. I'm not going to be able to do it without you."

"What are you talking about? You can still visit Ted the same as you always have. They aren't going to press charges, so everything is fine."

"No, Rose, it's not fine. It really isn't."

The pitch of his voice had risen to a more urgent tone as a minivan taxi came quietly to a halt in front of them, the hybrid engine barely making a sound. He bent uncomfortably and picked up his satchel, tossing the bag across to the floor on the far side as the door slid automatically open.

Rose felt herself becoming a little annoyed.

"Why not, Wally? You're not making any sense."

He stood silently for a moment and then allowed the driver, who had come around to assist him, to take his arm and, putting a hand across his back to prevent him falling backwards, manoeuvre him awkwardly into the vehicle.

As the driver walked back around the van, Wally finally turned again to face her, his face set in a determined stare.

"Because the work isn't finished yet."

CHAPTER SIX — 1943

The low wattage bulbs strung from the tent seams allowed the small makeshift dormitory to be bathed in dull orange light. The injuries of the sprawling men ranged from glass and gravel puncture wounds to a cracked skull and third-degree burns. Two soldiers at the end closest to the exit were propped up, and one was speaking to the other in quiet tones.

He paused as an exhausted-looking nurse arrived and slid the chart from the foot of his companion's bed. The patient's right arm, shoulder, upper chest and neck were heavily bandaged and partially cast in plaster. One eye had swollen shut and was bruised to a deep purplish-black.

The young soldier who had been talking addressed her:

"Nurse Acres? How is he? My ears are still ringing so you'll have to speak up, sorry."

"Private Northam? It looks from the chart like Private Campbell has been fortunate enough to avoid infection from his wounds so far. They must stay clean, and his immune system must keep working."

"Thank God. Please, call me Wally. Any word about what happened?"

She replaced the medical chart and reached to take a pulse reading from Northam's wrist.

"Seemingly, the Germans seeded floating mines thirty miles upstream from the dam. They set the bombs on timers and calculated the travel time with such accuracy that they exploded inside the dam structure itself."

He looked incredulous:

"You mean, they killed their own men?"

"Well, we don't know that for sure, they may not have been aware that they still had soldiers at the dam. Anyway, I've seen plenty of instances of 'friendly fire' on both sides — it's a dirty business."

It wasn't clear as she moved away again, whether she had been talking about the dam incident or the war in general. Northam turned his attention back to the severely injured man beside him.

Edward Campbell ought to have been killed by the blast, but the pieces of wood, stone and metal that had invaded his upper body in that blinding, deafening moment had missed his major arteries by millimetres. It had taken army surgeons two and a half painstaking hours of probing to extract the fragments from his wounds and further minutes praying that they had left nothing significant behind. Pumped with a broad-spectrum liquid antibiotic and bound with absorbent poultice bandages he had been left to heal as well as God might allow.

Now awake for the first time and staring back at Northam through his one good eye, Edward spoke. His voice was hoarse and raspy, yet he was lucid.

"I can't feel half my body."

Northam scratched his brow at the edge of the yellowish bandage wrapped around his head and scowled.

"I'm sorry, Edward. I was so busy thinking about how much I didn't want to be in that god-awful situation, I forgot how much you and the other chaps were relying on my help. I don't even know if I managed to hit anything of value, I was so damn scared. Until the nurse just mentioned that the enemy bombed themselves into oblivion, I was sure my ticket was clipped."

"Ted."

Northam shifted uncomfortably to face Campbell more easily. He blinked.

"I'm sorry?"

"Everyone calls me Ted. Nothing you could do would've changed things. If it weren't us, it'd be some other poor buggars lying here. But I'm not gonna survive out here — maybe I'm a coward, or whatever — but I just don't have the guts to last."

Wally lay back in his cot and lit a cigarette, seeming transfixed by a stain in the canvas of the tent roof. He half-turned stiffly and waved at the stretchers on his other side as ash crumbled and drifted to the floor.

"See that first bed, Ted? That's Private Westcott there with half a leg suspended in the air. His parents will get to see their son again because of you. A coward couldn't have done what you did, and me — I'm not even supposed to be here. This wasn't my assignment, I was snatched and conscripted into this unit."

He looked back at Ted, but the heavy medication must have reclaimed its patient, and he was snoring gently with the same dry sound as when he had spoken.

⌘

On the fourth evening, they received a visitor.

Very little had changed apart from fresh bandages and the fact that Ted could now partially open his bruised eye. The purple colour had now faded to a yellowish-brown, and the white part of the eye itself was riddled with burst blood vessels.

Having little but each other for company, Wally and Ted had talked about their short lives, the jobs they'd had and their aspirations if the world ever recovered from the madness. A fast bond formed over this short period. Ted became comfortable enough to disclose fears that he'd been observed firing in the air instead of at the enemy.

"You know, Ted, a week ago, I'd have been one of the first to vote for leaving you to the vultures," replied Wally. "But even if I did get off a few good rounds in the fight, there's still a soiled pair of eighth-army shorts buried under the rubble of that dam with my name sewn into the waistband. I will never in my life berate another man for being afraid."

"I wasn't afraid. I think the adrenaline kicked in and I did what I thought needed to be done. I just couldn't live with myself if I felt responsible for taking a life."

Wally ruminated on this answer for a while, surprised by how quickly the black and white of a situation could become streaked with grey. As the afternoon wore on, Ted still regularly lapsed into sleep and Wally found himself drifting in and out of a light doze as the hours passed.

At around 2030hrs, Wally heard the rhythmic swish of uniform trouser-legs rubbing briskly together, and the tent-flap whipped aside as a dark silhouette materialised through the narrow opening.

A stern voice split the quiet hospital atmosphere:

"Private Wallace Northam?"

Wally raised his hand slightly as Ted rubbed at the eye he could see with. The speaker crouched down on one knee and looked at the two embattled youths as they scrutinised him with wariness.

"I'm Corporal Shoosmith, from Communications HQ. Northam, you're a hell of a long way from your post, don't you know?"

Wally slowly nodded, and his jaw set hard at the Corporal's

words.

The man flipped over the cover sheet on his clipboard and started reading from it, paraphrasing as his eyes flicked down the page.

"On the morning of the 11th of August, Private Wallace Northam was to have reported to Captain George Pottinger at His Majesty's Royal Army Recruitment Facility in Central London for transport and training at the WEC... subsequently found to have been pressed into service and sent to support Eighth Army efforts in the execution of *Operation Slapstick*... well, you know the rest. I have orders to pack you up and get you back where you belong."

Wally's eyes had closed in deep thought, and he wore a troubled expression. After a brief minute, he turned to Ted and said:

"Private Campbell, would you tell this man about your language skills."

Ted, fortunate that his injured face masked much of his bewilderment, slowly replied:

"I'm very good at languages. I graduated top of my class in French and German. I even chose to do an elective course in Japanese last summer for extra credit."

Wally turned back to the Corporal with a sudden air of officiousness.

"It's no mistake that I came here. My mission was to meet this soldier at the drafting office and bring him back to General Pottinger. He was to be assigned to the team before we both got caught up in this dreadful business."

Shoosmith was no idiot and had not been taken in by the story for a moment. He chewed his lower lip slowly as he regarded the burned and broken man with the pitiful voice in the cot next to Northam. His lips drew thin as he tightened them across his teeth in a humourless smile. At length, with a heavy sigh, he said:

"We'll be departing in four hours, so I suggest you both get as much rest as possible and have your personal effects ready to pull out by then. I'll go and see the doctors about getting you wrapped up and supplying the medicine you'll need to take on the journey."

The Corporal stood up and started negotiating his way through the obstacle course of cots and assorted crates to find someone to discharge the two young men into his care. After following his progress for several long seconds, Wally turned his attention back to his wounded comrade and winked, conspiratorially. Ted now sat at the edge of his stretcher, cradling his injured arm with the other, rocking gently forward and back. His cheeks were wet with tears.

CHAPTER SEVEN — 2019

"Oh my god, Ted, look what you've done to yourself! Wait, stay there a moment, Thea's gone to get some dressings, just hold your arm up for me... look at me! Look at me, Ted, this is no time to be fainting buddy, come on... that's it, here we go, let's just wrap it up in a towel, and we'll take you to get it cleaned up, OK? No, no need to say sorry, sweetheart — you didn't know what you were doing..."

⌘

"The cuts were deeper than we had first thought. Mr Campbell had to get four muscle stitches and sixteen to close the wound. There were signs of grazing on the arterial surface, but, well the truth is, he missed it by a whisker."

"We still don't know quite how he managed it — his hand ended up completely through the security glass, and I think he must have been so shocked at the window breaking he reacted by pulling his arm back through. It's the worst slice *I've* ever seen."

The registrar, a professional woman with an officious face, practical short haircut and perfectly manicured nails listened without interrupting. She finished jotting her notes down and pushed the incident ledger away from herself.

"Thank you, ladies. I'm sure I don't need to say how pleased we all are that you were able to respond so quickly and coolly."

She looked around the room, the same one that had hosted Ted's physical examination only a few short weeks before. The administrator of that previous meeting was also present and sat alongside as a quiet observer.

"We've got some tough choices to make, and it seems we have to make them with minimal delay. I can tell from today's turnout that Ted is both loved and well-supported, and we all want to make sure that any decision made regarding chemical restraint has only his best interests at heart. Ms Boyce: the most recent monthly report if you don't mind reading it out for us?"

Margaret Boyce, the unofficial senior carer of the group, stood and turned so everyone present could hear. She opened Edward Campbell's file folder to the top page and started reading the most recent entries.

"Nightly wander starts 19:35 Confusion/anxiety/fear. Could have pushed carer away easily but holds back. Talking to himself more and no longer whispering. Returned to bed 20:15.

...

...

Nightly wander starts 19:25. Confusion/terror/fear/undirected anger. Could have pushed carer away easily but holds back. Talking to himself constantly — very loud. Returned to bed 20:20.

...

...

Nightly wander starts 18:59. Confusion/terror/fear/undirected anger. Walking quickly away from staff as if escaping. Talking to himself constantly — very loud. Returned to bed 19:43. Approx. 1 hour to get to sleep.

...

...

Nightly wander starts 19:27. Confusion/terror/fear/undirected anger/panic. Barged (arms at sides) staff-member and nurse in a state of agitation, crying. Shouting directly at staff. Returned to bed 20:20. Trouble sleeping most of the night. Fine in the morning.

...

...

Nightly wander starts 19:01. Confusion/terror/frantic escalated state of anger/panic. Pushed himself into a corner (security exit, with glass) in state of agitation, crying. Shouting at staff to "Please keep away — I don't want to go there again, don't make me do it again." (repeated several times) When approached he closed his eyes and smashed his left hand against the glass and when he saw that it had cracked, he did the same again-"

She stopped reading and looked back at the lady registrar. "Well, you know the rest."

The registrar nodded, and Margaret Boyce sat down, closing the file.

The other woman stood and walked behind her chair, stopping to rest her hands on the back of it. She breathed in and out before calling for input from the group.

"Suggestions? Ideas? Theories? This isn't me saying you've all been doing nothing, but has anyone had a lightbulb moment in the last few days? Why does Ted do this? Why did he start only in the last couple of months? Is it something in his past, change in routine, a new presenter on his favourite radio station? Diet, medication, exercise regime, *anything*?"

The concentration of everyone was momentarily broken as Wally Northam, looking flushed, entered the room still wriggling out of his coat. Rose got up to assist him and led him to an empty seat. He sat down and quietly apologised for delays with the rail service.

The registrar pushed on.

"Thank you, Mr Northam, we were just at the point of seeing if any fresh ideas had surfaced about why Mr Campbell is having these ongoing episodes of trying to escape at night. I just need to point out at this stage, if we can't find a satisfactory and treatable cause for this problem, the next step is likely to be relocation to a more secure medical facility. There, Mr Campbell could be administered anti-psychotic medicines to try and bring his behaviour under control. It's an aggressive last resort, but we're out of options that the rest home can deliver and it's not fair to Ted to let him go on like this."

Rose sniffed more loudly than she had expected, drawing attention to the fact that she was not coping with the weight of this news very well at all. She apologised quietly, but other than this nobody spoke up. It felt to the majority like every avenue had been explored and dismissed, and that perhaps it was time to give up and start down the route of drug therapy.

Wally looked around the dejected faces and turned to the lady at the front.

"Excuse me," he said. "I know I'm not a popular individual with the organisation, but could I be permitted to look at the notes on these... behaviours, as you call them?"

She smiled thinly but asked Margaret Boyce to show Mr Northam the top sheet of reports that she had recently recounted.

He thanked them both and fished his spectacles out of his breast pocket. After a moment of squinting at the page, he stopped and rummaged around in his satchel until he found a reading glass. He held it up to the page and moved it back and forth in even strokes.

Mallory Bertenshaw — Ted's daughter — suddenly turned to Wally Northam and said:

"Uncle Wally, can I ask... about the inks you used for tattooing? Were they safe? I mean has tattoo ink ever been connected to mental illness or Alzheimer's disease, or anything like that?"

He frowned for a moment, lowering the paper and looking up at no-one in particular.

"I'd never rule out something I can't prove or disprove, Mallory dear, but I've always used the same brand that I used back in the army days. I get my supply from the local parlour, who still use it on people for vintage skin art today. They've never given me any warning about being toxic if that's what you mean?"

"No, I didn't mean anything by it, Uncle, just clinging on to any idea that pops into my head at the moment." Her Uncle reached across and rested his hand on hers for a few moments and then returned to reading the incident reports.

When nobody spoke for a further five minutes, a call to take a break was made and gratefully agreed to by everyone present. Wally Northam had only just arrived at the bottom of the report and closed it slowly. He muttered to himself a little and then a look of realisation spread across his face. He slowly turned to look over his shoulder at Rose Pickett, standing outside with her back to the wind and a half-smoked cigarette glowing redly against the background of her pale features.

He struggled to his feet and threw his coat around his shoulders, not bothering to wrestle his arms into the sleeves, moving with renewed vigour toward the door that would take him to her.

CHAPTER EIGHT — 2006

As Wally poured malt whisky over fresh ice cubes at the make-shift bar in his host's conservatory, Ted drifted, remembering the distinct air of confusion he had experienced on that day back in 1943, as Wallace Northam explained from his hospital cot.

"We're going to a place called Ramjas College — it's part of the Delhi University Campus."

"Delhi, as in India?"

"That's the one, yes, I don't know much more, except that we will be learning the specialist skill of codebreaking and code-writing to try and discover what is the truth and what is propaganda, on both sides."

Ted recalled the sudden stirring of hope he had experienced in the pit of his stomach at that moment. He'd felt compelled to speak up, irrespective of the consequences.

"Northam, we've only had these few days together, but I feel that we are kindred spirits and bound to become friends. Would you join me in a pact, here, today, between the two of us? An agreement never to kill another human for the purpose of war. These are only my own principles, but I promise to tell you if they ever change."

Northam had taken only a moment to consider Campbell's words before agreeing.

The appearance of a fresh glass of copper liquid under his nose snatched Ted back to the present. He pushed himself back in the chair with his elbows to a more upright position.

"I'm listening," he said.

"How many times did you let me loose with my tattoo gun on your pasty-white skin over the years, huh?"

Ted's brow creased, and he replied very slowly:

"Four... I guess, yeah, four times. One: the Turkish dagger you made out of the scar on my ankle in Delhi; two: that daddy-long-legs you tried to do on the other leg when we were both rolling drunk the week we found out the war was over."

Wally grinned broadly:

"It was supposed to be a Pegasus."

"Three: my bachelor party, when I got 'Beloved Edith' on my ribs, under the left arm; oh- and four: The *Enigma*."

Wally remembered the difficulty of tattooing both of their fore-arms. To celebrate the twentieth anniversary of breaking the elusive *Enigma* code, he'd designed a simplified image of the three rotors of the German code machine. It was yet another reminder of the shared experiences that bonded the two men together.

"So, Ted, here's what I'm thinking. You've got things you don't want to forget — important dates and relationships, etc. — so why not put them somewhere that you will never miss them, but no one else except you will know about it?"

Ted's hand gradually lowered his glass from his lips to his lap as he began to realise what his friend was saying.

"Are you suggesting that I should get the most important moments of my life... *tattooed* on my body?"

"Well, why not? I'd suggest using code, as you have for more of your life than normal writing. Every time you looked in the mirror, you'd be reminded straight away."

Ted spread his hands in consternation.

"Do I need to remind you how long it takes to do a tattoo on Yours Truly? I can hardly stand it for more than 10 minutes at a time, it's bloody painful!"

Wally tilted his head back and his mouth opened in a silent *ah*, remembering exactly how laborious the process had been each time. Both men sat without speaking for a while, each lost in his thoughts and musings.

They were startled back to reality suddenly as the sliding glass door from the house into the conservatory was dragged open and Grace, Ted's live-in housekeeper, emerged still wearing her coat and gloves. She wore a retro pair of winged cat-eye glasses from which her steely green eyes took in the details of the room instantly.

"Ted mentioned you might come over today, Wally. Will you join us for dinner?"

He regarded both host and surrogate hostess, then replied:

"If it's no trouble that would be nice, yes."

With a good-natured air of long sufferance, Grace, tugging her gloves off one finger at a time, replied:

"I'll empty the groceries, and then I'll get started. Is 'toad in the hole' all right with you gents?"

She disappeared back into the house.

Ted had remained only half-aware of the exchange — his eyes still fixed on the notes he had written about coping with dementia. Without looking up, he resumed as if Grace had never interrupted.

"We've been looking at this all wrong. This idea could work extremely well if we plan it out properly. But we'd have to write a list of the things I'm going to need to be marked, indelibly, on my person."

For the first time since arriving and starting up this line of reasoning, Wally experienced a trace of doubt. It showed in his changed expression, and Ted called him on it.

"If you live in an around-the-clock care facility, how are you going to know to look in the mirror? After all, they'll probably wash you and dry you and powder your bottom — you may never need to go to a mirror if you're so well pampered."

Ted nodded and shrugged. He tapped the page lightly with the back of the pen.

"Also, I wrote here about losing your memory in reverse, like your short-term memory first and long-term stuff later on. Some people don't know their own family when they visit, but they can tell stories all about the exploits of their unit during the war."

Another thought occurred to Wally as he sat looking at his hands, turning them palm-side up and back again.

"I haven't touched a tattoo gun in years, my hands are quite steady most days, but I'd hate to make a pig's ear of it."

As he continued to examine his fingers, he flexed and closed them into a fist a couple of times and then seemed struck by what he observed.

"I know what we could do!" He exclaimed. "Hand me that paper again, please."

He took the paper and pen and wrote two different symbols on opposite sides of the page in code. They looked to the untrained eye like the marks a baby might make if you gave it a pen and gently moved its hand over a piece of paper — very light and irregular. He handed the pad over to Ted and sat back, looking chuffed with himself.

Ted's eyes flicked from one side of the page to the other a few times. He read the symbols, translating them aloud, effortlessly, as he did so.

"Undress. Go to the mirror."

He looked up: "OK, I'll bite. Where?"

"Hold the paper up with both hands. Now imagine these symbols lightly tattooed into the web of your thumb and forefinger on the backs of both hands — they'd be hard to avoid at least somewhere in your day, right?"

CHAPTER NINE — 2019

Despite the sun's harsh rays warming the bricks and concrete of the Hannerton Rest Home buildings, the wind remained decidedly chill. Rose Pickett hugged her duffle coat tightly around herself, trying to bury her neck in the fleece collar. She looked up and saw Wallace Northam approaching with determination and sensed herself blushing. Feeling like a common road-worker with a filthy fag hanging out of her mouth, she quickly turned and tossed the cigarette into a nearby flowerbed and exhaled forcefully in a vain attempt to expel the odour.

Wally didn't seem to notice as he reached her. Taking her elbow gently, he said:

"Rose — please, you need to listen to me, I know why Ted's walking around at night. Can we go somewhere quiet to talk?"

Her eyes widened in disbelief, and she glanced around to see if anyone else nearby had heard what he'd said — nobody had. She pointed back toward the building and said:

"There's a spare office next to the meeting room, let's go there."

The room was devoid of character, had no windows or pictures on the cream walls and was furnished only with a small round table and two chairs on dull grey carpet. Rose pulled out a chair for the elderly gentleman and then sat down opposite him, hoping that this wouldn't prove to be the somewhat desperate ravings of a confused nonagenarian.

She waited a moment and then prompted him:

"So, why do you think Ted is waking up and wandering around?"

Wally reached into his jacket and pulled out the monthly report sheet he'd hurriedly stuffed there earlier. The paper was crumpled, and he did his best to smooth it out flat on the tabletop.

"I realised as soon as I read what he'd been saying and shouting at you when you tried to help him. You see, I've heard him when we were very young during the war, yelling the very same thing at the top of his lungs in his bunk. He used to have vivid nightmares back during the early months of the conflict. It was always the same nightmare too, although as soon as he woke up, he was fine — seeing me there and finding himself in a familiar place."

"Go on."

"Before I tell you, you have to promise to let me do what is necessary to get rid of the problem once and for all."

"What would you be able to do? You can't comfort people with dementia by telling them it's all a dream, it doesn't work that way Wally, I'm sorry."

"Don't you remember what I told you, the last time I saw you?"

She saw elements of the intense, pressing exasperation he had exhibited before he had been driven away from the last meeting in the taxi-van. She hoped it wasn't symptomatic of an unbalanced mind.

"The only way he will get peace is to let me finish this last tattoo. Look, here."

He turned over the paper and started writing a line of text in a font that she instantly recognised as being the same as the tattoo markings on the trunk of Ted Campbell's body. It was a short message, and although she couldn't tell for sure, it only looked like five or six words.

"Wally, I'm not going to promise anything. It's not my place to approve or reject such a serious request. I would *have* to ask the permission of the home to sanction a procedure like that."

"But you'd try, right? You'd *really* try, for Ted?"

Again, the pleading, plaintive eyes, searching hers for a spark of acceptance.

"I'd do anything to help Ted if I thought it was the right thing to do. But I don't understand getting another tattoo — why?"

He held up the report and shook it as if trying to get the meaning to fall from the page and lay neatly out on the table like scrabble tiles.

"I think he's having the same nightmare again, but this time when he wakes up, he thinks it is all still real. He used to dream that he'd woken up, injured, in the same army surgical hospital we were sent to near the frontlines. He was terrified that at any moment a surgeon was going to appear-"

"… and tell him that he had to get something amputated or have surgery without anaesthetic?"

"No. *To tell Ted that he was all better and fit to be sent back to the front.*"

⌘

The news of a possible cause of Edward Campbell's episodes engendered an optimistic hubbub amongst the reconvened meeting members. The lady registrar had to ask for quiet so that Rose Pickett, standing quietly and patiently, could continue with her bold claim.

"As I said, I have discovered that this behaviour relates to some historic nightmares that Ted used to have during the war. It's quite well documented that dementia can take many years to affect long term early memories, so it's not unreasonable to understand why, only now, he is starting to have these dreams again."

Noting that her words appeared to be sinking in, she went on, but with less certainty.

"Now that we have a spark of understanding the root causes of this, maybe we can consider what alternatives to try instead of taking the route of chemical restraint. Nobody wants to be pumped with drugs if there are other ways of dealing with a problem."

She paused and swallowed, realising even as the words were on the tip of her tongue that she ought to be censured for using such unprofessional terminology.

Wally Northam, feeling that Rose was going to back down and avoid speaking up for him, decided that the time had come to do so for himself.

"You have to let me tattoo Ted again!" he blurted out.

The room was silent for a moment as the delegates processed his words and then erupted in an explosion of chaotic vitriol. Shocked, Rose felt the sudden turn in tide knock her so psychologically hard that she was forced to take a step backwards and sit down painfully into her seat. Everyone had started talking at once, unleashing their disapproval upon Wally, who had been the perpetrator of this false and unkind scenario of hope.

The rest home administrator was scathing in his reproach toward the frail old man that sat slightly hunched at the table.

"Mr Northam, we warned you about this weeks ago — I seriously thought you'd taken it all on board and started acting with proper respect for your friend. Apparently, I was wrong, as you seem to have no concern for his welfare at all with these ludicrous antics!"

Wally bowed his head and took his face in his hands.

Ted's daughter, Mallory, had also clearly withdrawn her support for Wally. In a screeching tone, she now asked why he had once again brought this obsession with his ridiculous tattoo art to such an important meeting, especially given how much Ted's future depended on it.

"Just *please leave*, why don't you!" she shouted across the table at him.

His hands were visibly shaking as he took them from his face and wrapped them around himself, hugging his shoulders. Wally seemed to absorb the onrushing tide of negativity like literal waves during a storm.

The registrar held up her hands to regain control of the room and said calmly:

"I'm afraid we've heard quite enough of this now," she stood, turning her back to the room as a mobile phone appeared in her hand. She pressed a single key and lifted the handset to her ear: "Security, we have a meeting attendee who'll be leaving, thanks."

In the momentary stretch of silence that followed, Wally's weak voice broke through.

"It's the only way — it's the only way for Ted to be at peace with himself. Rose, tell them it's the only way..."

The door opened, and the rest home security men quietly entered and walked over to Wally Northam's seat without even asking if he was the person they'd been called to remove.

Each took an arm and tried to lift him, but he seemed to have gone as limp and heavy as a sack of potatoes. As they set him back down to get a better grip, he slid forward off his seat, his chin striking the edge of the table as he disappeared beneath it.

Chairs scattered as those sitting next to him made room for Rose to crawl under the table and kneel beside him. His face seemed frozen in a fearful grimace, and his eyes stared upward, sightless as Rose saw her fear-stricken face reflected in them. She placed a trembling couple of fingers against his neck and felt nothing. Sliding back on her haunches, she sat up, looked slowly from one enquiring face to another.

"He's dead," she said, feeling a hot tear start to run down her cheek as the words came out.

CHAPTER TEN — 2019

Rose hoped that this solution was going to be enough. Was the writing that the late Wally Northam had scrawled on the underside of a piece of paper the whole message, or just a fragment? She'd fought long and hard with herself about going behind the backs of the powers-that-be and knew that, if she failed, it would be her job — and no doubt prison.

But she couldn't face sending a man she professionally loved and respected off to lose his last remaining grains of dignity to drug-induced limbo and ignominious death. Compared with even the slightest chance of overcoming his fears and returning to a life of attention and respect from people who cared for him, she'd finally made her choice — consequences be damned.

She'd had to cut things very fine, waiting until Ted once again was rostered into her care for the night. Another two days and he was due to be moved to a specialist unit situated many miles away in Wales.

"Almost done... hold the light a bit higher... that's better, thanks."

The tattoo artist, in his fifties, was a staunch admirer of war veterans. He had listened carefully to Rose as she explained the profound emotional effects that the war still had — and that he could greatly help a war hero in his time of need. He had refused to accept the envelope of money she offered and insisted that the job was both an honour and its own reward.

At the head of the bed, Rose held Ted's hand firmly and talked to him in reassuring tones. He lay still, maintaining his composure apart from the occasional wince as the tattoo gun went just a fraction deeper.

The machine was loud. It didn't just buzz — it whined, chattered and rattled noisily. The walls and ceilings included thick baffles of soundproof insulation, but Rose still expected police officers with batons, tasers and handcuffs to burst in at any moment.

They had been working for approximately 20 minutes, taking care to pause and swab the area with a mild antiseptic and a topical anaesthetic.

At long last, Rose heard a satisfied grunt from her co-conspirator. He stood back and pulled down the surgical mask she had insisted on him wearing.

"Let's get cleaned up," he said, "you'll wanna make sure no one sees a drop of ink anywhere in this room, or you'll be down the road."

Rose had draped the bed and surrounding floor with plastic sheeting, and she knew that the most challenging task — disposing of the evidence — still lay ahead. For now, she just wanted to make sure Ted was going to be fine. The tattoo artist spoke again.

"Let's get him up, I need to wrap the new area in plastic to keep it clean — don't forget, you'll have to sponge-bathe him yourself for a few days until it can come off."

She put an arm around Ted's shoulder and helped him to a sitting position with his feet dangling over the side of the bed, as the artist wound what appeared to be plastic food wrap several times around the old man's waist.

"There you go, not too tight, I hope?"

As the elderly man heard these words, his breathing appeared to change, coming in shorter bursts. His cheeks flushed, and his eyes started to dart about.

"No…," he said. "No, this can't be right, I don't want to go back again — don't make me do it again, *please.*"

Rose called out in a harsh whisper to the artist, who had picked up his tattoo gun, intending to start to disassemble it.

"Hey, can you bring me that wall mirror hanging over the vanity unit there, please? Hurry."

Ted started to writhe against Rose's attempts to prevent him from falling off the edge of the bed, and she tried to redirect his attention.

"Ted, look at me: we're not going to send you away, OK? Look, look here in the mirror."

Like a plug had been pulled somewhere out of sight, the elderly resident stopped cold as his eyes caught sight of the new message that had appeared. His breathing slowed, and his shoulders slumped. Without warning, he started gently to cry.

Aware of Rose still holding the crook of his elbow, he reached out hand over hand up her arm and, pulling her close, he buried his head against her, huge sobs wracking his delicate frame. She held him for a while until he calmed a little and then gently pushed him back to look him in the eyes.

"Is everything OK now, Ted?" she asked.

He wiped his eyes with the back of his hand and nodded, turning again to look at the message for fear it had vanished, but it had not. He then looked up at the silhouette of the artist, a mere shadow behind the mirror he held up.

"We did it, thank you, Wally."

Rose helped him to swing his legs back onto the bed and under the cover, making him comfortable against the pillows. She dried his face with a fresh cloth and looked at the serene smile he now wore.

"Wally explained to me about the codes you used in the war and the tattoos to help you remember," she said, "you were very clever, both of you. But can I ask you, Ted, what does this last message say? I really want to know — can you tell me?"

She held the paper up to the light for him to see, and his eyes sparkled as he reread the line.

"Of course, I can tell you what it says."

He reached out his finger, following the line as he recited:

"The war ended; your hands bear no blood."

SÌOL CLUARAN

1

"No-one really knows when and how life began."

I can tell from Charlie's expression that this is a frustratingly un-satisfactory answer.

We sit together on an outcrop of rock about 450 feet above sea level, overlooking the shoreline of the fiord. It's late afternoon, but we feel warm, wrapped in blankets and wearing woollen beanies to protect our ears from the coastal wind.

Charlie and I have been climbing regularly to this spot. It pro-vides solitude and quiet time to think about the situation. I can't imagine what he's been going through — losing both parents in the crash — but I've decided to wait until he's ready to bring it up, poor bairn.

It's never exactly quiet when surrounded by over three million acres of native forest and all the bird and animal life that goes with it. Added to this, we crashed in about 100 feet of water, so there's noise from sea-birds, insects and the waves.

I say we hit the water, but fortunately, our momentum allowed the ship to grind its way through the shallows and up onto the shore. Now it's rested on its left side with the bottom hanging out like a gutted salmon. We scraped a mountain peak on the way down, spilling the contents of our hydroponics bays and oxygen recycling system over a few hundred acres of mountains and valleys.

From up here, we can see the camp down at the threshold of forest and beach, and the little graveyard we dug, a short walk to the North.

There are only ten plots. The ground was incredibly hard to dig, and most of us have suffered injuries of one sort or another. So we buried families together — mostly couples, like Charlie's folks. They'd been trapped in the cabins closest to the nose of the craft. It was crushed in by the rock face that finally arrested our journey.

By profession, I am, or I *was*, a botanist — the only one from a litter of seven born and raised, all of us, in Aberdeen, Scotland. My parents were both in oil and gas, so we enjoyed a comfortable upbringing. My brothers and sisters didn't wait long to leave the Shire and head to where all the excitement was in the big cities like Edinburgh, Glasgow and London.

Of course, they're all dead, and in the end, my career choice to work with plants inevitably saved me. I can't say that my fate has been much better, with everything that's happened.

But Charlie is still waiting for an answer better than the one I've just given him.

2

His question was: "How did we get here?"

He really is a beautiful boy. He has the most piercing light green eyes under a wild shock of reddish-blond hair. His expression is always one of calm deference, and while we were still aboard, I remember the deep dimples that formed when he smiled at his father's jokes.

I haven't seen the dimples since then.

He has so much hair that some of it is sticking out from the front of his hat. It gets in his eyes, but he doesn't seem to notice. I don't have children of my own, and I don't even know if I can explain it at his level, but he deserves for me to try.

"Do you know how internet URLs always start with www?"

He scowls at me and immediately replies: "World Wide Web."

I feel a bit sheepish, hoping that he doesn't think I'm treating him like an infant.

"Well, Ok, good — but have you heard of the wood wide web?"

He frowns and shakes his head, picking small clumps of grass from the cracks in the rock he perches on.

"The best way for me to describe the wood wide web is… it's like the internet for plants — all plants, like trees and bushes and ferns and even seaweed."

"You mean, plants can talk?"

"Kinda, but not the way we do. They send signals to each other with, I suppose, a feeling that the other plants can notice and feel too."

I can tell he's trying to process my words, but there's no light of comprehension switching on yet. Continuing my line of reason, I pose a question back to him.

"Did I have to talk to you two days ago, when we both decided to run like a couple of squealing girls back to the camp?"

"No."

"And which one of us started running first?"

"Me."

"How did you know to run?"

"Um, well, I didn't know to run, but when I saw you looking scared as well, I thought we must've been in danger from a bear or something, so I just ran."

"And what did it turn out to be?"

"A kiwi bird."

"Right!"

We grin at each other, remembering the heart-pounding moment when we'd heard a rustling sound from the forest undergrowth nearby and acted like idiots.

For the first time since crash-landing in this barren place I see, just for the tiniest moment, the dimples appear in his swelling cheeks as he chuckles to himself.

"There aren't even any bears in New Zealand, I remember learning it at school. Those birds only come out in the night, so we should've done a selfie with it."

He's looking again at the little row of crosses in the distance, obscured slightly as evening mist rolls in from across the water, and his smile is quickly dissolved. He tries to hide some inconvenient tears by blinking furiously.

"Is that how they tried to kill us — by sharing their feelings?"

"That's what Lady Sylvia and I thought — she was my boss, you know."

He's nodding, and I can tell he's thinking about the adjacency of her grave to his parents'.

"My mother said she saved us all," he turns his face to me, no longer bothering to fight the waterworks, "on the *Sìol cluaran.*"

3

The day after her 52nd birthday, Sylvia Robertson inherited an immense legacy from her billionaire uncle — Lord Francis Worley Robertson. She conceived and built *FloWeR* - one of the most revered hydroponics centres in the world.

FloWeR's massive glassy domes nestle in the Cairngorms National Park like jewels in the face of the Scottish Highlands.

As I ponder Charlie's statement, I wonder if they're still there.

"She did," I say as I fish a clean tissue out of my jacket pocket for Charlie to wipe his tears, "it was her idea from the beginning. She used every penny of her uncle's money to build a colony ship to escape and find another world."

I see a snapshot in my head and am briefly transported back to the whirlwind events of the past few months — like seeing a movie poster and remembering the whole film in a matter of seconds.

Summer of 2020. Lady Sylvia, an intimate group of friends and colleagues, a heartbreaking vow of confidentiality beyond the walls of a small conference hall.

"Over-confidence in the ability to master nature led men to split an atom... and thus the scales tipped irrevocably against homo sapiens."

For the first time, at a sub-atomic level breaking the barrier between seawater and freshwater to the vegetation on land, the plants of the world had become a unified network. She delineated that nuclear activity had been a deadly catalyst. Through millenniums of signalling danger from pests and infection, a new cleansing solution aimed at humanity had been circulating since the 1940s.

And we just got worse.

Deforestation, erosion, mountains of discarded plastics, decimated insect populations, rising tides and temperatures, extinctions, water contamination, air pollution and ozone depletion sent alarm messages through the underground pathways of the plant network.

I remember feeling shocked and numb as she delivered the final verdict:

"The Director of the Cooperative Institute for Research in Environmental Studies has privately confirmed that humanity has less than 30 years before they become extinct."

And amidst our disbelief and sorrow, she revealed her olive branch. Plans were underway to construct a secret colony ship, one capable of taking less than 100 souls on a generational journey to find another world and make a fresh start.

The ship would be complete with hydroponically grown plants. These would be isolated from the network, living symbiotically and harmoniously with their human carers.

It took 17 years to complete the *Sìol cluaran* so named from the Gaelic 'thistle seed'. A seed that we hoped would drift through space and land in the fertile soils of a new world. Fear of discovery was constant, and the burden of knowing the fate of humanity while being impotent to help — infinitely worse.

We launched on Valentine's Day, 2041.

We left various monitoring devices behind to check atmospheric conditions and, while they lasted, media transmissions. We listened in misery for eleven years. It was like keeping vigil over a dying relative — times 9 billion.

Cities... winked out, and eventually, voices ceased. Music continued for a while, in morbidly looping playlists until finally replaced by static, white noise.

During a solemn ceremony, a solar-powered probe was launched into orbit. We hoped it would remain for thousands of years to tell the tale of man to any who would listen. And as we prepared to depart, an engine failed, and we plummeted back to the ground.

4

We see a familiar beacon flashing up at us from the camp in the fading light and Charlie gathers up our flasks and books. He scans the cover of the volume I brought with me, *An Examination of the Mycorrhizal Network.* There's a cover illustration of a cartoon mushroom, using an old-fashioned typewriter.

"Is it the wood wide web thing?"

I nod, take the book and stow it in my pack, starting to explain as we head for the path down to the camp.

"Yes, it's just the fancy name for it. Basically, all the plants have tiny fungi growing on their roots, and the fungi are like wireless modems, passing email messages back and forth between the plants. Shine a light down there, will ya?"

He fishes out a torch and, still listening intently, stays just ahead of me as I continue.

"They share news about health, or warnings of attack from diseases and pests. They can even use the network to send nutrients to younger plants of the same species — like feeding their children — but they can also send poisons to kill neighbours they don't like."

"Is that why the trees here seem to be in groups of the same kind — sort of like herds of animals that stay together?"

"You're a smart kid."

We're almost at sea-level again, and I stop to fill my flask from an icy mountain stream that trickles down to meet the deeply gouged furrow leading up to the wreck.

"How did they kill all the people?"

"We think maybe they leached chemicals into rivers and streams, which weren't harmful to any other creatures on the planet except us. It was almost as if plants could naturally do what scientists had tried to accomplish for decades, targeted genetic modification."

"I don't know what that means," says Charlie as he unlaces his heavy boots outside the tent we now share.

"Well, just that only humans got the diseases and allergies that killed them — no other animals were harmed."

"But we're back on Earth. Are we gonna die too?"

I shrug my shoulders — I don't have the answer.

We begin preparing for sleep, neither of us relishing the taste-less, freeze-dried emergency rations we are forced to eat.

Later, lying in my bunk, I reflect on the initial exploratory missions that found evidence of shipboard hybrid plants that had taken root and flourished at an astonishing rate. Could it be that a message from these spacefaring relatives has restored the network's faith in man?

I reach for the flask of water and take a long, cool drink.

FEAR

The fear is real. I know I'm in a world of trouble despite not knowing the exact situation, and I must escape.

I hear them, standing two beds down as if they think that I can't tell they're talking about me. This might be some sort of other-worldly, extraterrestrial hospital, and I might well be a patient, but I can still hear like a bat.

The problem is, they talk in such gibberish I can barely make out what they're saying. I've heard them refer several times to *the patient in bed number 27*, but I am confused by the name they use as it makes no sense to me whatsoever. It's a woman's name, like 'Harriet Williams' or something. And I hear phrases like: 'proper procedure' and 'can't make an informed decision until...'

I've already worked out that I'm suffering from a concussion and a certain degree of mild amnesia. However, I'm not crazy, I still have my reasoning and observation powers, and I've always had a very analytical mind. Big pieces of my memory are entirely intact, which is why I think my fear is utterly appropriate to the circumstances. Either they're going to torture me for information they think I've got, or they're deciding whether I'm expendable enough to kill.

I am a fighter pilot. I'm privileged to be one of the 'chosen few' of Tactical Air Command to train and fly the *F-104 Starfighter* supplied by the United States since the early 60s. We didn't know at the time, but their generosity sprang from an ulterior motive. It wasn't until New Year's Day 1976 that we discovered what that was. I'm now part of a top-secret anti-espionage task force that remains on high alert to fight any threat to national security.

Wait: here they come again. I have to stay sharp, even if I am incapacitated. I've tried to file away in my mind any details of conversations I've had with them in the hope that, with luck, if I ever escape, the command team might be able to use it to find a chink in their armor.

I hate the way they pretend to be concerned over my health. They even have actors coming in and claiming to be my daughter and granddaughter. I guess they don't realize that I'd rather *schtup* the granddaughter who looks about my age, but never in a million years the hag troll they've chosen to play my little girl. Proof positive, I guess, that their intel leaves a lot to be desired.

The usual nurse that comes leans over me.

"How are you today, Mr. Roosevelt, feeling more like yourself?"

I pretty much say nothing unless severely provoked, so I stay silent and sullen.

A new character steps forward, dressed to look like a doctor or maybe a psychiatrist.

"Mr. Roosevelt, I'm Doctor Segers. I specialize in helping war veterans deal with the traumatic experiences associated with active duty. I understand you feel that the staff here in the hospital are not who they say they are. Now, I know sometimes it is easy to get a little confused in an unfamiliar environment such as this, but perhaps you've had time to relax and realize that you are surrounded by people who love you and want to help you?"

I'm feeling calm and under control until this reiteration of insult to my family.

I remember like it was yesterday how I got to spend just two weeks with Marien and our new daughter before being flown to the Military Flying School in Jackson, Mississippi. She'd only just given birth, and my CO felt I should get to spent some time with my new family to give me something to fight for. My baby girl is the most gorgeous flower on the face of this Earth, and even if I never get to see her again, I'll fight tooth and nail to preserve her future freedom.

Bringing my family up again forces me to cry out.

"Stop trying to poison my mind with your lies and propaganda! I'm one hundred percent loyal to my country and my people. Now you take those vile... *animals* out of here and leave me be, I won't tell you anything!"

I feel myself spitting, but I don't care, the message seems to have gotten through. They've moved away again and drawn the curtain around my bed. I hear them murmuring amongst themselves, but seeing my real family again spurs me on, and I feel renewed vigor to get back to them at all costs...

⌘

"Ms. Roosevelt, this is the last opportunity for you to reconsider this decision."

"I understand, Doctor. And I won't be changing my mind. I love my father as much today as I did when he first returned from the internment camp thirty-seven years ago. I want this for him to preserve his dignity, instead of rotting here in a demented state, not knowing who he is or who we are. Did you know that he was a pilot? Captain Gerrit-Willem Roosevelt of the Royal Netherlands *Commando Tactische Luchtstrijdkrachten*. His experiences helped formulate today's standard anti-espionages procedures. I just can't stand to look at him like this anymore."

"He still has periods of lucidity though, Ms. Roosevelt — you've said so yourself."

"Look, we're not having this conversation again, Doctor. This is the Netherlands, is it not? And euthanasia is legal, is it not? And as the legal guardian of my father, I have the right to decide that it is in his best interest to be euthanized. So I would appreciate you signing the approval form and letting me get out of here and on with my life."

The fear is real. I know I'm in a world of trouble despite not knowing the situation exactly, and I must escape...

⌘

EndNote:

Some license has been taken with this story. The euthanasia laws in the Netherlands at the time of writing still allow the responsibility of choice to remain solely with the individual, not their guardians. So even if a patient previously indicated that they wanted to be euthanized under a specific set of medical circumstances, if at a later time in any conversation they indicate the contrary, then the procedure is nullified.

UNHOLY CHAPEL

CHAPTER 1

If the air-conditioning system had been less efficient, motes might have danced in the rigid beams of light that shone on the matte-white wall behind SAC Ray Holden. But no expense had been spared to create the pristine, state-of-the-art conference facility in the heart of the J. Edgar Hoover building.

Holden stood at the head of a sprawling round table, at which were seated 22 agents in the employ of the Federal Bureau of Investigation.

The meeting was a secret one. This special arm of the Bureau was established back in '71, not long after its formation. They served to handle cases that fell outside the jurisdiction of federal or even international law. It went without saying that each member had been screened beyond doubt before becoming one of the chosen few.

They looked with patience and professional intent at their Chairman, his sun-hardened, uneven skin dark against the whites of his steely gray eyes. His immaculate dark brown hair was tinged with flecks of salt-and-pepper. His usually kind visage was streaked with a severe frown, and his eyes flicked from one face to another as if measuring the mettle of the team before deciding whether or not to proceed.

He took an innocuous manila folder from under his arm and gripped it in both hands.

"I call your attention now to Dossier number 17: ALBRECHT KAPPEL."

He looked up, but there were no expressions of recognition.

"This *Schweinehund* represents the pinnacle of Nazi sadism and violence."

The picture of a man in his later years flashed up onto the wall behind Holden. A handsome man with a square jaw and a full head of silvery hair tidily groomed. It was only a bust, but it was plain to see that he was dressed in an expensive ruffled shirt, dinner jacket, and a silken cravat. It was the same face that appeared on the polaroid photograph clipped to the front of the folder in Ray Holden's hands.

Holden looked over his shoulder at the larger-than-life portrait and continued:

"While the Reich managed to keep his record of vivisectionist torture under strict wraps, we have been able to uncover stomach-turning evidence of his behavior during the final 18 months of the Fuhrer's reign…"

The screen now showed an early colored film with no sound, apparently shot from a secret location, perhaps a suitcase, moving through a hospital ward of restrained and undernourished prisoners-of-war. Some were unconscious, some screaming in terror, and others stared vacantly as if all humanity had been removed and only a shell remained.

"… the kind of stuff that will give you nightmares for the rest of your life if you let it."

Close-ups now — bleeding ears, eyes, mouths, and scalps. Some with unclosed surgical openings to exposed internal organs, severed limbs, hyper-extended joints bound at unnatural angles. Mutilated genitals, hands, and feet. Horrific burns from head to foot. Tubes dripping poisonous and corrosive chemicals into bodies that had come to look more like rotting cadavers. And the inevitable trip to the outside where hundreds upon hundreds of discarded corpses lay piled in mass graves.

The scenes were replaced by familiar legal courtroom images from the well-known Nuremberg trials held after World War Two to address war crimes.

Holden's officious drone resumed:

"He acquired refugee status here in the United States 30 years ago. He is untouchable — maintaining his innocence for decades and even under the deepest scrutiny at Nuremberg, he managed to avoid so much as an unpaid parking ticket. Geneva couldn't touch him, and neither can American Law. So that's where *we* come in."

Apart from the flat screen section, the room was completely round, mirroring the table at its center. A door opened at the farthest point from Holden, the only entrance, and a woman entered. She was a much older operative with silver hair gathered into a bun at the back with regulation clips and wore a typically monochrome black and white trouser suit. She was pushing a file-room trolley with one large document box resting on the tilted shelf.

Wheeling it ahead of her, she arrived at the head of the table, where Holden removed the lid and deftly turned the box upside-down on the table.

A flickering look passed between Holden and the woman, making it clear to any who saw that she already knew the contents and was utterly complicit with the details of the meeting.

"Thank you, Special Agent, please take a seat."

As the woman moved to the one remaining empty chair in the room, Holden lifted the box straight up and allowed the files inside to stand in a more-or-less upright stack. He put the box and lid back on the trolley.

"So, as I was saying, that's where *we* come in. We are going to make sure that this abomination disappears in a manner befitting his crimes. Anyone wishing to abstain from this operation may leave now."

Still, nobody moved or spoke.

In a sweeping motion, Ray Holden gathered the stack of dossier files up, and casting from left to right seemed to create a perfect fan of documents that ended up resting, one-per-person, in front of each agent present. In unison, they reached forward and dragged the records toward themselves. Without opening them, they each rested a hand on their file and looked again at SAC Holden.

He held up the small remote unit that controlled the digital projector for the first time. The gesture seemed to silently indicate that this was the last chance for anyone to leave if they were having second thoughts.

"In that case — prepare to step outside the realms of real humanity and pray that you aren't tainted by the evils of the duties I must now assign to each of us... and may The Lord have mercy on our souls."

With a flourish, Holden clicked the remote button and turned his whole body around to face the screen.

"OK, here's what we know about him."

CHAPTER 2

The click of the remote control button not only started the next scene rolling from the projector but also dimmed the room lighting by about half what it had been.

It was like being transported instantly into a surreal antique theatre. Very faint 1920s-style pianola music could be heard from the tiny mono projector speaker, and a black and white film of a theatre stage gradually coalesced into view.

The characters' movements were typically jerky and robotic as was the norm for early film cameras, and scratches, dust, and hair blinked on and off the surprisingly clear picture.

A young Albrecht Kappel stood, arm outstretched, delivering a speech to a rapt audience, his admiring colleagues waiting in the wings. As he concluded, the audience jumped to its feet, applauding wildly and throwing bunches of flowers at him. He gathered several of these, bowing numerous times and walked waving one-handed until the curtain eventually dropped and obscured him.

Throughout this piece of vintage cinema, Ray Holden's briefing continued:

"For two decades, before the war, Albrecht Kappel was considered one of Germany's finest actors — both on the stage and the silver screen. He played almost as many leading men as Douglas Fairbanks Jr., with just as much adulation from the peoples of Germany, Austria, Switzerland, and other European nations."

The screen went dark, and slowly the lights in the room returned to their former brightness. For the first time, the agents who had been sitting stolidly at the table shuffled and stretched, shifting their positions slightly.

Ray Holden started very slowly to meander from his position at the head of the room, placing one foot deliberately in front of the other as he passed behind each chair.

"Over the next four months, we are going to learn how to function as a well-oiled art-film crew with a reputation for producing black, seedy movies about violence and unstable human behavior."

He stopped moving and noted that an initial shimmer of interest had passed amongst the group — raised eyebrows, head tilts, sideways glances. He went on:

"Our biographical script about a famous US serial killer being illegally brought to a bloody end by vigilante FBI agents will be irresistible to him. We will tell him he looks identical to the man the lead character is based on," he raised an index finger as if to add his masterstroke, "plus, he'll believe all of the agents coming and going on set are just extras!"

There was evident warming of the room to the forthcoming assignment as a ripple of assorted snorts and stifled throat-clearing passed through the group.

Ordinarily staid, Holden began punctuating statements, clasping his fist in the other palm.

"We must learn to appeal to this scum-bag's ego. Flatter him, draw him out on his career. Dwell on the gore in the film, the power that the main character had over his victims, the reckless, remorseless way he butchered them!"

Heads nodded. Holden came three-quarters of the way around the table and turned to walk at the same slow shuffle in the opposite direction.

"I have been authorized to offer him up to ten million dollars. He must come to believe he was born for the part and that the rebirth of his career is now within his grasp. Untold strewn corpses are crying out for us not to fail them. And now-"

He stopped, turned, and reached out his hands to rest on the shoulders of the agent seated in front of him. The man did not jump or show signs of alarm. He had swarthy skin, jet-black hair, a pencil-thin mustache, and a deep five o'clock shadow. His eyes flashed like polished wet obsidian.

"Meet Assistant Special Agent in Charge, Grigor Erasovic. Because of his secular background, he has been chosen to be our dark, brooding, genius movie director. When I am not on-location, you will take orders from ASAC Erasovic."

Erasovic did not stand; he merely scanned the room and picked up his folder, tapping it on the tabletop to straighten its contents. His pleasant baritone had no hint of anything but the most typical Washington white-collar executive accent.

"We'll meet here again for preliminary briefing in three days — read your profiles thoroughly, and I pray for success upon our endeavor. Dismissed!"

CHAPTER 3

Kappel's residence was located near a small rural town about seventy miles from the heart of Bangor, Maine. A long, winding driveway flanked by eastern white pines and the occasional red maple tree led to a dated but well-maintained colonial homestead.

Agent 'Trigger' Haynes and Special Agent Maggie Potter chatted about everything but the purpose of their visit as they navigated the steep, loose-graveled road. They'd deliberately left their guns and jackets behind in the government-issue sedan and opted to appear as open and friendly as possible.

Haynes, still relatively new to the Bureau and not long out of the academy, wore low-rider jeans with a Norton motorcycle belt buckle and a crisp sky-blue linen shirt, open at the collar. He wore leather cowboy boots but had them tucked under the boot-cut Levi's. He also carried a black zip-around document satchel under his arm.

Potter had opted for an above-the-knee pencil skirt in faded pastel green, soft-leather low-heeled walking boots, and an off-white singlet and jacket combination. She also wore a straw hat and aviator sunglasses.

They heard no sound from the house as Haynes rang the doorbell, and so he knocked loudly and then stepped back to wait. A cool breeze brought the scent of pines down from the sprawling forest behind the homestead. He closed his eyes and took some deep, appreciative breaths.

The door opened noiselessly, and it wasn't until the person inside spoke that Haynes blinked them open again.

"Good afternoon, can I help you?"

"Mr. Kappel?"

"Yes."

Haynes held out a business card.

"I'm Marlon Campbell, and this is Julie Fratelli. We've been asked to come and see you personally about a career opportunity."

The old man looked back in confusion.

"Career? I'm 83 years old — are you sure you have the right house?"

"Mr. Kappel, it doesn't often happen nowadays, but we represent a company that is making a film about a famous American criminal called Eugene Eustace. Have you heard of him?"

Again the old man looked blank and shook his head.

"Can't say that I have, no."

"Well, the thing of it is, sir, we've been asked if you'd consider coming out of retirement to play the part of Eugene in our film. Didn't you used to be an actor before the war?"

A sudden look of comprehension began to form on the face of the man they'd come to visit.

"A lifetime ago I was an actor in Germany, yes. But why come to me? Like I told you, I'm too old for dressing up and reciting lines."

Time for the woman's touch. Maggie pulled off her sunglasses and gave Mr. Kappel the full benefit of her lovely gaze.

"Mr. Kappel, when Marlon said: 'it doesn't happen very often' what he was meaning is that you are quite the spitting image of this character, Eugene Eustace. You look exactly like him, and when he died, he was only one year older than you are now."

Trigger Haynes piped in again: "We're authorized to offer you $750,000 plus expenses to travel with us to Washington to shoot the film. And we'll put you up at The Four Seasons for the duration of the project."

The old man stepped out of his front door, reached for a cane that rested there, and beckoned his visitors to a picnic table under a drooping black willow. He looked up into the branches.

"This tree was already grown when I bought this place 30 years ago. It's probably as old as I am, but it got a blight some time and never grew more than this — it makes a good shade."

He stroked his chin and sized-up the two younger people sitting opposite.

"I'm long in the tooth as I have heard people say here, and most of the movies I see from Hollywood these days are, well..."

He didn't finish the sentence but wrinkled his nose in distaste.

Maggie grinned.

"There are a couple of things, Mr. Kappel. First, this isn't Hollywood, it's an independent film and a factual one. Secondly, this is a unique chance for you to do what every brilliant actor dreams of. Leading hero roles are a-dime-a-dozen. But to play a truly evil villain garners much more kudos in the acting world."

"And is this character so evil? I didn't read about him or see anything in the news."

"Eustace murdered 27 young married men in cold blood, sometimes in rather nasty ways, and the hell of it is, he got away with it on a legal technicality because the investigating officers contaminated the crime scene. He went on to commit two more murders before a team of vigilante FBI agents captured and tortured him to death. Nobody in the Bureau would confess or expose their colleagues. This was back in the eighties."

"Such behavior for men of our age. How did you come to choose me? Mere similarities aren't everything in film."

"Are you kidding?"

She unzipped the document pouch and showed him printouts of websites and magazine clippings.

"You're a legend in the film aficionado world. People hold seminars and discuss your methods at conventions. Obviously, you're a very private man, but even younger generations who fancy themselves as film historians, rave about the films you've been in."

A barely noticeable change came over the old face, and the man seemed to straighten his back and grow an inch in his seat.

"5 million."

Both agents looked at each other as if they mustn't have heard right.

"I beg your pardon?" Maggie managed to splutter out.

"If I'm the only man who looks like this Eustace, and you were willing to come all the way here from the capital to ask for me specifically, then you've been granted leeway to negotiate. So I want 5 million dollars to do the job, plus accommodation and expenses, as you say."

Albrecht Kappel was no longer a wizened pensioner, creaking along on a walking cane with dim vision and a shaky, weak voice. He was suddenly a cold, steely businessman demanding his worth in no uncertain financial terms.

Trigger stood up with a flushed red face and, as rehearsed, began hotly: "What the f-"

"MARLON!"

Maggie stopped him dead and pointed down the driveway.

"Why don't you go back and cool off in the car? I'll be down shortly."

Clenching his teeth, Trigger Haynes started down the road, leaving Maggie and the chameleonic Mr. Kappel under the tree.

He turned his attention to her, and she met his gaze with equal strength.

"You're right, of course. I can negotiate, but not that high. I was told I could go to 3.5 million. You wanna sign the contract right here and now on a firm 4, and it's a deal. I can vouch for my boss, he'll agree, so what do you say?"

She knew she had him.

CHAPTER 4

The first day of filming consisted of the usual bustle as equipment was unpacked from nearby warehouses and vehicles. Catering stands started spreading out their wares and finding nearby power outlets to start heating coffee and tea. Rows of trailers began lining up to accommodate the talent during the periods between filming scenes. People ran to and fro, and some stood in little groups ticking off clipboard lists and making urgent mobile phone calls.

ASAC Erasovic, in his role as Miles Morgan, independent film director, had called an emergency cast meeting outside in the morning sun under the shade of a large table umbrella. Iced teas had been brought to them, and he addressed everyone:

"Welcome, welcome, and welcome. It's day one, and I want to get down to business straightaway. As you all know, financial constraints mean that most movies are not shot in chronological order — so I want to do the final death scene first."

"You mean the scene where the FBI ties me up in an abandoned warehouse and beats me to death?"

Kappel sounded enthusiastic at the prospect.

Erasovic went on:

"That's right, but there's an additional element we hadn't bargained for."

The DOP frowned.

"Oh?"

"Because of the strict censorship laws here in the US, I intend to continue filming afterward to show Albrecht wiping the blood off and maybe bending a few of the foam baseball bat props. Then we can show it during the credits at the end. The international version won't need it, but here my hands are tied, I'm afraid."

Kappel smiled, looking warmly around the table as though reassuring a bunch of novices.

"We understand. That should be quite entertaining."

One of Kappel's co-stars, dressed already in his costume as an FBI agent, looked at Albrecht with an almost deviously conspiratorial expression.

"Not as much fun as being beaten to a bloody pulp, eh, Mr. Kappel?"

"My dear boy," the aging actor replied, "I'm merely a tool in the hands of the director. I simply do what needs to be done. No scene is more or less important than any other as far as I'm concerned. You, too, will come to appreciate this, in time."

CHAPTER 5

Tendrils from the off-camera smoke-machine curled past the outstretched legs and feet of actor Albrecht Kappel as he sat with his hands cuffed and chained above his head to the cold brick warehouse wall.

Detritus of every kind were strewn liberally about to give the appearance of decay and abandonment. There would be cutaways of rats and spider's webs later. An untidy stage of torn damp cardboard boxes framed the scene, and the character of Eugene Eustace languished at the center.

The make-up artist had done a brilliant job with his tousled hair, a bruise on one cheek, and a generally disheveled appearance. Kappel himself could not see much as set lights had been placed to create a high-contrast look with a deep black background and cold, harsh illumination on him as if Eustace was being held in the spotlight of several powerful FBI flashlights.

For continuity, cameras had been placed at various focal lengths and locations to capture the entire scene in every take. One had a full close-up of Kappel's face, squinting against the glare. Another shot over the shoulders of some FBI agent stand-ins to give perspective and context. They wielded an assortment of baseball bats, 2x4 timbers, and batons.

The director's voice cut through and silenced the room.

"Let's get a take on this thing and see how it looks in-camera. Remember you 'agents' — for the opening dialog, you just look menacing — like Rottweilers being held back until it's time to be let go. Andy?"

The script supervisor, standing ready to feed lines to Kappel for him to respond to, called out that he was ready.

As each department responded that they were set for a take, Grigor Erasovic looked intently at the small digital monitor that held the actor's face in the frame. At his shoulder, Ray Holden stood, his face grim. Despite the loose-fitted exterior appearance of his suit, underneath his muscles felt taut and quivering. The success of this mission depended entirely on the convincing realism of this shot.

Erasovic glanced up at him from the director's chair. He nodded back.

The clapper loader stepped into the frame and said in a clear voice:

"Dishonorable Death — scene forty-three: take one."

He closed the clapper with a satisfying snap and pulled it out of shot.

Miles Morgan's voice rang out:

"Action!"

⌘

Andy, the script supervisor, played the part of the accusatory leader of the FBI vigilante group with enthusiasm, making it easy for Albrecht Kappel to respond as the psychotic character he was portraying. As the exchange drew to a climax, Andy gave the word for his minions to exact their execution.

They read the scene a couple more times, and then the shooting stopped for a very short resetting of reverse camera angles and resumed almost immediately.

The cleverly designed foam props landed blows all over the re-strained actor's body, and various ingenious machines under his costume sent out realistic spurts of stage-blood. Fake compound fractures poked through its ripped fabric. He supplemented the carnage with appropriate growls, cries, screams, and final weak moans as the agents stepped back to examine their handiwork.

Everyone stood silently waiting, experienced enough to know not to make a sound until the recordist gave the director the signal that he had enough extra for a clean crossfade.

"Cut," shouted Miles Morgan.

He turned to the man next to him and said in a low voice, "Is the documentary crew ready?"

Holden nodded.

"They're set up along the walkway leading to the outside, there's room for the actors to stand maybe five abreast as they leave."

Erasovic turned and belted out an announcement:

"Brilliant work, everyone. Hopefully, we got it in three takes, but we'll leave the room set up just in case. That's a wrap for the day, and can I just pause to say what a god-damn Hercules performance from our star today. Albrecht, take a bow; you deserve it!"

The now released Kappel stood and basked in the ovation of his fellow cast members.

As the applause died down, the director went on:

"Don't forget, as you walk out, play it up for the documentary cameras — we need to keep the censors happy."

⌘

Later that evening, ASAC Erasovic and SAC Holden sat in the comfort of a large operations truck watching back footage on a large monitor.

Kappel, surrounded by the other actors, was making his way along the plastic-covered walkway from the warehouse set. He wore a towel around his shoulders and was using a separate wash-cloth to wipe away the gory make-up that covered his face and was beginning to mat his hair. He smiled and laughed with the others as they waved their baseball bats triumphantly about, bending them and bopping each other in mock battle.

The hand-held footage had a very amateurish quality about it as if some high-school film fans had been allowed to come on set and do a few behind-the-scenes shots.

Erasovic took a drink of black coffee and clicked his mouse over the rewind icon a few times.

At length, he stopped on a freeze-frame of Kappel's face half-turned in a smudge of motion-blur.

He said in a humorless tone:

"I don't really have the stomach to do this again unless you think it's not good enough?"

As Ray Holden was about to reply, he was stopped by the appearance of the mature female agent who had delivered the Kappel dossiers during the initial briefing. She marched across the room and handed him a newspaper selection.

Special Agent Abrams was a private person, not one for conversation, yet a fountain of knowledge on matters of politics and law. Despite her age, the years had been kind, and the rigorous bureau training had helped her maintain good posture and fitness.

"Thanks, Abrams. Take a seat, help yourself to the coffee and sandwiches."

She took a chair, a little further back from the editing console, as Holden began flipping through each newspaper, pausing for a moment on each headline as he went. As he finished each one, he handed them to Grigor Erasovic to look over.

When he'd reached the last edition, he turned again to the flickering still image of their target.

He looked over at the older woman, still regarding him with sullen anticipation as she cradled a coffee cup in both hands, and suddenly gave her an uncharacteristic smile.

"They're works of art. Can you see that they make it to his trailer and hotel room over the next couple of days?"

She stood and collected the pile from Erasovic, who had stacked them tidily on a stool next to his chair.

"No problem," she said and walked to the door. She paused and looked over her shoulder at the two men watching her. She flicked her eyes at the screen and added:

"Will it work?"

Ray Holden and Grigor Erasovic exchanged affirming glances and Holden, reaching over to turn off the monitor, replied:

"You know what? I think it will."

CHAPTER 6

Kappel woke from his mid-afternoon nap with a start. He could have sworn he'd heard a knock on his trailer door. He swung his arthritic legs awkwardly until he was sitting and with a grunt stood up.

He reached into the small electric icebox and deposited a couple of large cubes into a glass. He poured a double Jaegermeister. It had been his beverage of choice since the 30s, and he lamented somewhat the syrupy nature of the American version. He was sure the drink of his youth had had more of a raw bite to it.

He left the liquid to cool down in the ice and walked to the door. When he pushed it open, he saw no-one walking away or reaching out to knock a second time. The lot appeared unoccupied except for a couple of technicians fixing a soft tire on one of the neighboring buses. He looked down at the heavy-duty crate in front of the door. It served as an extra step to help him get into the trailer more easily. There were a couple of local newspapers lying on the crate.

Realizing the effort required to stoop down to that level, he was about to give up and leave them where they lay, until one of the headlines caught his eye. Fetching his cane, he eased himself down to the ground outside, turned around, picked up the papers, and stepped up into the trailer again, closing the door behind himself.

He placed the chilled glass on the table and, as an afterthought, reached for the bottle. He squeezed himself onto the sofa behind the counter and opened the first paper, *The Washington City Paper.*

A side-bar showed some of the leading articles for each internal section. Under entertainment, there was the headline: 'Veteran international star Albrecht Kappel elevates independent Eugene Eustace Biopic to another level. — Page 13.'

He dragged the other broadsheet across the table to himself and skimmed down the page. There it was: 'Auteur Director Miles Morgan's extraordinary casting coup — Kappel's jaw-dropping performance leaves crew speechless, according to an industry insider.'

His eyes gleamed, and he took a long, slow sip of reddish-brown liquid. He felt like a phoenix stretching for the first time, twisting his stiff neck slowly from side to side as the alcohol warmed his throat and seemed to relax his whole body.

Then another animal image drifted into his mind — he suddenly felt like a cat, tossed from an upstairs window, and landed firmly on its feet.

⌘

It took three and a half weeks to complete principal photography. Then the second unit director dropped off his footage, and 'Miles Morgan' went into hiding to start the laborious process of editing and collaboration with the sound and music departments.

He requested the cast and crew to be available for one more week in case of urgent reshoots if they were identified in time.

Meanwhile, SAC Holden had been posing as an FBI consultant, making sure the procedures and jargon in the film were authentic. He was also running damage control for numerous nervous staff-members.

Approached by a young agent one evening, Holden realized the fragility of the situation they were trying to maintain. The man knocked on his door and seemed at first reluctant to enter. He fidgeted for a few moments, and it became clear that he had probably drawn the short straw from a bunch of his peers to visit the SAC.

"Folsom, what is it? I haven't got all day."

The young man glanced around himself and climbed inside, taking a seat on the narrow couch.

"Chief, a number of us are having doubts about whether we've got the right guy here. I mean, Kappel... he's an amazing man! He's generous, thoughtful, and kind, and he treats everyone on the lot with dignity. He just doesn't react when we talk about war and horror stuff. Are you sure-"

"That's enough, Agent Folsom!"

Holden leaned over and closed one of the perspex windows he'd opened earlier for ventilation. He looked sternly at agent Folsom and almost snarled at the poor young man.

"Did you think I showed you the footage of what he did at the Guggenheim Experimental Hospital for a few laughs? I seem to remember you looking pretty green afterward. Don't forget that, and don't forget either: Albrecht Kappel is one hell of a good actor!"

"Yes, Sir."

The chastised agent looked drained of color, and the stark reminder had been a much-needed slap in the face.

"I needed that, and sorry. I'll make sure I remind everyone how easy it is to get sidetracked."

Holden's phone rang, and he picked it up without another word to agent Folsom, who quickly departed, closing the door silently behind him.

Maggie Potter shared her job with Trigger Haynes, her junior partner, but she shared her life with Aiysha Burkett. They weren't allowed to be assigned together on individual cases, but as this was a department-wide project, they worked on it in different areas.

Burkett, of Nigerian descent, was taller than Maggie and a disciplined athlete. She worked with Agent Abrams in the data team as an IT specialist.

All four colleagues sat that evening in wicker chairs on the roof balcony of the apartment block that was being used as a final filming location.

"This is gonna drive me to early retirement, and I can't be the only one."

It was Haynes who had spoken. His brow was creased in a deep frown. He continued:

"How can I play executioner to some elderly dude, who hasn't shown a scrap of racism, bigotry, or even a bad temper, and then come home and try to make a baby with Gill without thinking about what I was doing during the day? And what will I tell the kid when it grows up and asks what I do at work? It's *insane*."

Aiysha Burkett sighed.

"We're all feeling the strain, Trig, every one of us. Last week it was me starting to crack up, right, babe?"

Maggie squeezed her hand and nodded as she threw an empathetic smile at Haynes.

Abrams sat quietly smoking a cigarette at a slight angle to the rest of them as she watched the younger agents and listened to their worries. She wore a thick woolen sweater against the chill of the night air. Clearing her throat slightly, she offered some advice:

"If it makes it easier, Agent Haynes, I'd suggest you imagine your future wife and child with that animal standing over them, rubbing his hands together. Those kids in the Guggenheim movies were all somebody's son or daughter, or parent."

Haynes and the others shivered at the somewhat callous, calculating way she spoke.

The problem was, they knew she was right.

CHAPTER 7

Excitement filled the rooftop set, as 'action' was called on the last scene to be shot for 'Dishonorable Death — The Eugene Eustace Story.' Champagne bottles stood ready to be opened amidst tables filled with expensive hors d'oeuvres. The whole crew had gathered behind the cordon ropes in eager anticipation of the impending wrap party.

Two FBI agents sat in a rooftop café comparing field notes. Their faces showed suitable concern and concentration. They were oblivious to the fact that the target of their investigation, Eugene Eustace, sat right at the next table smoking a slow-burning cigarette. One of them was speaking:

"The crime scene investigators say his pattern and MO will lead him right here to Manhattan."

His partner put down his drink and wiped his mouth.

"Six hundred miles and twenty-seven dead — I hope they catch the *psycho freak* this time!"

The camera made a long, slow zoom from the two agents right to the hand that held the cigarette as it crushed it into a slice of heavily-iced cake. The camera remained fixed on the piece of cake as smoke drifted from the hole for what seemed an eternity.

"Cut... and... that's a wrap!"

The whole roof erupted in cheering and applause as Erasovic held his hands up and waved to everyone. He managed to shield his eyes as the familiar 'pop' of a champagne cork split the air, and a gush of fizzy liquid splashed in his direction.

The party had begun.

In all his years as an agent, special agent, and now as SAC, Holden had never found it so hard to maintain character. He'd seen the substantial emotional toll this assignment had taken on his team and had several times had to reassure, remind and reiterate to them the true goal of the mission, the tragic and bestial crimes they were setting to rights.

The only actual alcohol flowing was the one bottle of champagne from which Kappel was being plied, and the reserve bottle of Jaeger that he would undoubtedly move on to. The rest of the crew were drinking grape juice, zero-alcohol beer, and green tea.

Holden reminded himself to push for commendations all round; they had been through hell and kept professional the whole time. And by this time next week, it would be all over.

Before Kappel had had time to finish his second glass of champagne, Erasovic had expertly maneuvered himself to the actor's side and was soon joined by Holden. Both had effected a jovial mood for the conversation.

"How do you think the film will turn out?" Kappel was saying as Holden sidled up to them with a merry grin.

Erasovic shot a glance at Holden and back to Kappel.

"It's fantastic…"

Albrecht Kappel tilted his head.

"It sounds like you wanted to say: 'but,' there for a moment, Miles."

"Albrecht, I'm thrilled with your work on this picture, but when I viewed the dailies for the final scene, I wasn't happy with the lighting or the lack of good close-ups on your face. I just wish I had another chance to-"

Kappel exploded:

"But why *not* reshoot it? It's only a day's work! You've kept the warehouse set intact. I'll stay if the rest of the crew can!"

In faux support, Holden immediately backed him up:

"Man! I'm so glad you said that. I've been feeling the same way since we started but was too afraid to say. Albrecht, you were acting your lungs out, and we kind of took the performance for granted."

Kappel slammed his palm down adamantly.

"If that's what it's going to take, let's do it — reshoot it."

Erasovic breathed a measured sigh.

"Really? I'll talk to them all after the party — I'm sure they'll do it."

The three men solemnly shook hands, and Kappel moved off to try his best to convince an entire film crew to do what they each already knew they were going to agree to.

⌘

"I'm not going to like this part either, am I?"

The girl's negative posture — arms tightly folded, jaw thrust out, chin on chest and eyes staring up at the glowing cinema screen — spoke volumes about what she'd thought of the last sixty-five minutes of her life that she was never getting back.

The boy sitting next to her was quietly thinking about the $6.50 he'd wasted on this chick. He hadn't realized that when hot girls toss their heads and say: 'horror, yeah, I love to be scared,' what they mean in reality is pretending to be frightened in the jump-scares of Beetlejuice and Sleepy Hollow — and then making out.

Of course, that had still been his end-game, but the rushed and rather ineffective gore of the murder scenes in this flick had soon put paid to any chance of an excellent preliminary make-out session. Pity, she had a killer rack and had seemed pretty up for it at his sister's dorm party the night before. He sighed, scraped at what was left at the bottom of his popcorn tub, and started watching again.

It looked like the final scene anyway. The camera was tracking through an abandoned warehouse with junkie needles, discarded shoes, broken machinery, and cracked concrete that oil had leaked over at some time. Vermin scuttled amongst the paper and boxes.

There was a clank of chains, and the camera changed tack and zoomed toward a far wall, drawing up short at the body of a man with bound ankles, his wrists cuffed and stretched painfully above his head to a steel ring embedded solidly in the brickwork.

He recognized the antagonist, Eugene Eustace — the 'Cuckoo Killer' — surrounded by angry, vindictive-looking FBI agents with an assortment of blunt weapons. The suspenseful music came to a sudden stop, and the spokesman for the group started reading out a list of his crimes against married men and states where they had lived.

The boy stole a sideways peek at his companion.

"Yep, I'd say this isn't gonna be pretty," he whispered.

CHAPTER 8

The usual hubbub of the film crew was noticeably absent as they robotically arranged the scene, set the lights and cameras, and prepared for the final appearance of the 'star.' Once set, Erasovic, with a grim nod from Holden, asked for Albrecht to be brought from his trailer.

Three of his co-stars from the weeks of filming had volunteered to be the ones to bring him in. They had encouraged him to stay in the comfort of his temporary residence and have his costume, make-up, and binding of feet done there, so he could 'get into character' and be carried straight to the set ready to start shooting immediately.

When he was ready, the nervous agents lifted him, two at his shoulders and one at his feet, and began the short walk to the adjacent warehouse. His weight was less than the burden on their consciences and hearts. If any of the intel on this guy had been flawed, this could go down as the biggest FUBAR in bureau history — if it ever saw the light of day.

They laid him gently down over the taped 'X' on the ground and made sure that he could lean somewhat comfortably against the brick wall. Erasovic came forward with the handcuffs, and Kappel extended his arms like a gentle lamb as the other man attached the restraints, secured them to the wall, and then stepped back. Everyone stepped back. There was suddenly a palpable space surrounding the small elderly man.

Dry throats swallowed, nervous teeth ground, and stomachs tightened in the surrounding pall.

"Right, everybody: places for the final death scene — take 2. Oh, by the way, Kappel," Erasovic didn't even pause for breath, "there's someone I'd like you to meet."

Kappel squinted up at the contre-jour human shape that had stepped out from behind the director. It was that guy that had been shadowing Miles Morgan almost every day since the shooting began, the consultant from the FBI.

"Albrecht Kappel: I am Special-Agent-In-Charge Ray Holden of the Federal Bureau of Investigation."

"Yes, Mr. Holden, I recogn-"

"ALL of the people you see here are agents of the FBI on a special covert assignment, not filmmakers or actors. The assorted weapons of execution you see them holding now are not props, they are very real. We are here for one reason and one reason only."

Kappel blinked back, at the silhouette, still without comprehending, but his brow started to crease into an expression of wariness.

"*ALBRECHT KAPPEL...*"

⌘

A sly grin had started to appear across the boy's mouth, and he subconsciously dug his nails into the soft arms of his seat. Without taking his eyes from the screen, he tilted his face toward the girl.

"He's gonna get it now, I wouldn't watch if I were you."

She, not wanting to give this repulsive guy the satisfaction of observing her discomfort, responded by putting her elbow on the rest between them and placing a hand under her chin. It allowed for quick access to place it over her eyes if needed, without being obvious.

A burly agent on the screen had stepped forward from the gathered mob and began to pronounce sentence:

"Eugene Gordon Eustace..."

The shot changed to an extreme close-up of the murderer's defiant face.

"... In the final court of humanity, you lie here to be judged and executed for the inhuman atrocities you committed upon your fellow man. Murders for which you have never been brought to justice until now!"

She saw his eyes begin to widen with terror as the words sank in.

The camera panned across the faces of the agents in the front row. They told a story of realizing things had been taken too far, and now passed the point of no return.

⌘

Irrespective of age, the knees of every agent felt like jelly. They fought down a rising panic, some on the brink of snapping and trying to make a run from their sickening duty.

And then, it happened.

Albrecht Kappel, the helpless, friendly old man, shaking in his handcuffs on the floor in front of them, exploded like a cornered animal. He snarled, and flecks of saliva sprayed outwards as he spat his words at the shocked onlookers:

"I vomit upon your kindergarten ideals! Those creatures weren't people — they were less than vermin, less than the spores of mold we eradicate with bleach from our homes. What I did to them was only what we needed — for us and all future generations!"

His head oscillated back and forth like a grotesque fairground clown, searching futilely for a sympathetic face. His voice rose to a shriek.

"It was art — you think my acting career was something? Bah! They were just raw material for my playground, and I experimented with relish! And even though the time was cut short, THOSE WERE THE GREATEST YEARS OF MY LIFE!"

Freed from all apprehension, like automatons, the avenging agents came forward and started to rain blows down on the prisoner's body, moving with prolonged, slow deliberation toward his head.

⌘

Imploring petitions for mercy cut through the horrific sounds of fleshy impact.

"No- no, wait- stop… Aaaargh!"

The voice was muted as a blow struck the murderer full in the mouth.

Retching, the girl turned and buried her face in the boy's chest.

"I can't watch this, please!"

The young man's jaw had dropped at the hyper-realistic violence of the scene, like nothing he had seen so far, in this film, or any other.

"Oh man, that looks so totally real…"

He found himself cradling the stricken girl's head against him, realizing that she hadn't deserved this.

In an instant, the screen cut to black, and a sinister final music chord struck, a sparse ringing piano chord that announced implacable doom.

The reeling audience looked about at each other as if seeking mutual comfort in the proximity of strangers.

The music chord had faded, and a gentle, almost music-box-like melody had started to play as the first credits started meandering up the screen.

Behind these, a new picture was congealing and taking unfocused form. Movement. People walking toward the camera. It was the actors, including Kappel looking exhausted, but jostling each other and laughing.

The boy shook the girl's shoulder gently.

"Aah — I see! Look at the credits, honey. He's fine, see?"

Kappel was wiping blood out of his eyes and sharing the amusement as his colleagues pretended to be supermen, bending the foam baseball bats and pieces of wood. As the credits continued, the picture faded to black again, and the rest of the orchestra took up the soundtrack theme.

The girl pushed herself back into her seat and watched for a few seconds. She leaned forward, gathered up her jacket and purse, and stood up. The last he saw of her was a brief reproachful glare from the end of the row before she stormed off toward the exit.

EPILOGUE

Abrams, Burkett, and Haynes leaned over the balcony of the now-vacated rooftop staring out across the Washington skyline. The two younger agents were sharing a freshly rolled joint. Maggie Potter was still at the Bureau having a debriefing session and wouldn't be back for a while. The green-screen sheets that had been put up to allow Washington to become Manhattan had been taken down, and the muted sounds of traffic and birds drifted up from the city.

It was still light, although the sun struggled to filter through the haze of city heat and pollution that pervaded the upper-levels of residential apartment buildings.

Haynes was talking, and his voice sounded hollow and thin.

"I almost didn't go through with it. If Kappel hadn't…"

"You did what had to be done, don't beat yourself up about it."

"Is the world always so black-and-white to you, Agent Abrams?" He asked.

"When it comes to the klan, yes and wife-beaters can kiss my ass too. And nazis…"

She reached across and, to his surprise, took the pungent cannabis from him, holding it between thumb and forefinger. She gently blew on the end of it until it glowed. Then, putting it in her mouth, she pulled up the jacket sleeve of her left arm, turning her hand palm-up.

She scratched at a very faint but unmistakeable tattoo. Haynes' eyes bugged at the sudden revelation.

She took a long drag and let it out slowly as she looked at her watch and said:

"It's time. And you can call me Esther — when we're away from work."

They all turned and sat in wicker chairs around a small table with an ashtray and an AM/FM radio. Abrams switched it on. The third news item came on, read by a very disinterested-sounding announcer.

"The body of the little-known actor, Albert Chapel, was discovered under a bridge near Oak Brook, Chicago early this morning. He had been brutally mauled in a manner that the FBI suspects copycats the way his final character role in 'Dishonorable Death' was bludgeoned and killed. Never married; Chapel is not survived by any known living relative. And now in sport, it seems likely that weather will be a deciding factor for teams when the new season starts-"